1 | The Plug's Daughter

The Plug's Daughter

Nika Michelle

names, characters, entities, places, people or incidents are entirely coincidental.

Acknowledgements

I have to give thanks to God for giving me life and the gift of writing first and foremost. Also, thank you to my parents, siblings, family and close friends for always supporting me. You know who you are.

Thank you Leo Sullivan and the entire Leo Sullivan Presents/Sullivan Productions family.

Also a special thank you to my promoters Sharlene Smith and Sharon Bel. See how your names start out the same? I knew it was something special about you ladies. Thank you for everything.

To all of the authors and book clubs on social media that support me, thank you. I would name you all, but the page count won't allow it. Lol. Much love.

Last, but not least, thank you to all of the readers. I would love to name all of you who support me, but as I stated before, I have to keep it short. *wink* No love lost though. I did post a status on Facebook on 9/17 asking for readers to drop their names for this page. I have to have this book to my publisher by 9/18, so I'll add all of the names I can. If I didn't mention you, you have my sincere apologies. You support is greatly appreciated and doesn't go unnoticed.

Special shout out to Charles Lynch, Pat Johnson B (thank you for test reading), Shannon Joshua, Shatika Turner,

Alexandra Branham, Chalane Moore, Christine Denise, Jacole Laryea, Tahysha Livestobefree, Nikki Burden, LaLa Hilton, Linda Marie Mota, Robin Goodman, Tami Orr, Sharon Simmons, Danielle Michelle, Elvisia Hickson, Kenisha A. Johnson, Cheryl Hayes (I love the purse), Lacresia Evans, Kiera Northington, Pam Williams, Tammy Jernigan, Umeki Brown, Ladee Bern, Latora Pittman, Hope Msmaewest Jones, Lashan Denise Cooper-Davis, Clarine Andujar, Cassandra Glenn, Kenia Michelle, Lorriane Tillman, Quaran Owens, Debbi Kowalik, Michal Howard Moore, Andrea Williams, Latarsha Cates, Wilona Arango, Tonischa Craig, Shanicia Jackson, Christy Silver, Nicole Prillerman, Keela Lynch, Natasha Vaughan, Denise Fuller, Sunnie Robinson and Janelia Brooks.

If your name wasn't mentioned please charge it to my head and not my heart. Thanks again.

Prologue

Keenyn

The loud, banging sound woke me up immediately.

"I know she in there nigga! Open the fuckin' door before I shoot it down!" The voice was deep and raspy.

'Oh fuck,' I thought as I grabbed my glock nine from under the sofa cushion.

On my way to the door I thought about how shit had played out. The only thing that I was guilty of was developing feelings for a woman who was supposed to be off limits to me.

I peered through the peep hole and confirmed who was knocking on my door like the Feds. Although I hadn't been prepared for the intrusion, something had told me when I first heard the noise that it was him.

After putting the gun in the waist of my jeans I opened the door. He stared at me with eyes full of malice.

"Where the fuck she at?" He asked.

"Who you talkin' bout yo'?" I played dumb.

"You know who the fuck I'm talkin' 'bout nigga!" His gun was out and he held it against my temple after closing the door behind him.

He was alone which was a plus, but I was sure that he'd disturbed the neighbors. I could only hope nobody had called the cops.

My face was balled up in anger. He just didn't know. How the fuck was he at my spot with that bullshit?

That nigga cocked the gun as his fiery red eyes stared me down. "You fuckin' her?"

You really wanna take it there?" I asked as I glared at him. "It ain't what the fuck you think it is."

Shit what the hell did I have to lose? Before he could take a breath I had my gun pointed at his head too.

"What is it then motherfucka?" Spit flew from his mouth and landed on my face. That shit infuriated me for real. He was surprised that I had pulled out on his ass too. "You either fuckin' her, or you ain't."

"I'm just tryna protect her," I said without flinching.

He let out a sarcastic chuckle. "Protect her? I can do that shit myself nigga!"

"Well, obviously you ain't!"

He smirked at me and then let out a grunt. "What the fuck you protectin' her from then?"

I shook my head. "You won't know if I kill you." My menacing eyes shined fearlessly.

"Nigga, you gon' make me kill yo' ass," he spat.

"Either way you won't know the truth," I said.

The hatred that was in his eyes earlier turned into curiosity. He was still mad, but he wanted to know what I was talking about. I didn't say anything right away. Shit, he still had his piece to my head and I still had mine to his. She would be mad at the both of us if it all went left. More than likely she'd feel betrayed, not to mention that she'd be in pain. I couldn't help what I felt though, so if it had to be a war, then so be it. I was in love with her and I would die 'bout her. The only thing was, he would too and I knew that shit. Either way I looked at it, I wasn't lowering my gun as long as his was on me. I didn't give a fuck. When it came to my life, no man's life mattered and I wasn't afraid to shoot.

Chapter 1

Keenyn
Two Weeks Earlier

"Man, all I want is a three five. You know I'm good for it," JJ's begging ass was always trying to get a freebie.

I shook my head and sighed. He was my home boy and although I thought about doing it, I wasn't going to ever make any money fucking with niggas like him.

"Look nigga, I'm gon' front it, but you better pay me back. Shit, I done gave you enough trees to plant a fuckin' forest. I know you tryna get some pussy from Felicia and shit, but you better make it happen with a couple loud ass blunts. Stretch that shit. I know you got some cheap ass liquor at the crib and some fruit juice. Bitches love sweet drinks and shit. If you got some Limearitas nigga you in there."

JJ laughed as I passed him the plastic baggie and then put it to his nose for a smell. "You a stingy, smart mouthed ass mufucka."

Yeah, I did have a way of stinging a mufucka with my words, but stingy I was not. "Stingy? Nigga, if I was stingy yo' ass would be leavin' here empty handed. Get the fuck out my crib. My girl's on her way over anyway."

My face was balled up as I kicked that nigga out of my spot. Why the fuck was he always broke? Probably because he was a fucking trick who didn't mind spending dough on random broads. We had grown up together and shit, but he was starting to become a financial burden. Not only did he want some free weed every other day, but that nigga was all up in my closet trying to cop an outfit for the night. For real nigga? Go get a fucking job, or a real hustle. Ain't no chick going to be satisfied with that bogus, fugazzi ass bullshit. The nigga was always claiming to be on, but he wasn't making no funds. How the hell could you be on and you couldn't even afford to smoke? Flexing ass nigga.

JJ stood up and rubbed his chin thoughtfully. "You be on some bullshit man."

"You still talkin' nigga? I need yo' ass to get to walkin' out my shit." I was laughing, but I was as serious as a heart attack.

He put the small baggie of bud in his pocket and headed toward the door. "A'ight nigga. I'll holla at you later."

I didn't say a word as he closed the door behind him, but I got up to lock it. After that I headed to the bathroom to get right for my bae Elena.

* * *

As I stared at my image in the mirror, I couldn't help but be feeling myself. I was a nice looking nigga with swagga. Not only that, but at the age of twenty two, I had a lot going for myself. At 6'0 even, 190 pounds, I was built solid as a mountain, fuck a damn rock. My workout regimen was deadly and I executed it at least three times a week. A nigga stayed in the gym. My body was my temple and so I watched what I ate too. It was important that I drank a lot of water to maintain my clear, milk chocolate complexion. I only ate fish and poultry. No beef or pork had ever been in my system. My late mother didn't eat either of them and neither did I.

With closely trimmed facial hair and a neat, low haircut, I tried not to stand out amongst my peers too much. Most niggas were into the thick beards and shit, but I believed in keeping it clean and crisp. I was taking classes at Clark Atlanta University in Criminal Justice, which sounded crazy because of my extracurricular activities. I needed to be on top of my game though. However, I didn't plan to be in the game forever, even if I was only in it on a small scale. I only sold weed, and that was because I didn't want to indulge in anything that would get me too much time if shit went the wrong way.

I was a careful nigga though. My clientele was very exclusive and I didn't fuck with random niggas and shit. Not just that, but I only sold an ounce or more at a time, nothing less. I copped my product from the plug that I'd known since I was seven years old. When my mother died from pancreatic cancer I was only four. I lived in Raleigh, North Carolina with my mother after my parents had split up.

My mom, Cherice Gaines, was a beautiful woman who had loved me unconditionally. When she got sick my life changed drastically. At first she was a vibrant twenty six year old woman, but then she wasn't anymore. She'd been a heavy drinker since her teenaged years and it had affected her health greatly. I knew that she was drinking even more after my father had left us when I was three. He decided that marriage and a family was too much for him, but he still provided for me. He'd even come pick me up every other weekend out of the month and I spent summers with him in Atlanta.

My mother had moved in with my grandmother, who was a registered nurse, after their split. I had everything I wanted at my grandma's expense. She died in a car accident when I was four and after that we lost everything. We ended up living with relatives in not so good neighborhoods. That was my first real exposure to the streets. Not even a year after that my mother was dead and I knew that depression and loneliness had contributed to it. A few days after my mother's funeral my pops, Kenard Gaines, took me in. He didn't work an honest job. He was a street hustler who did street shit and his ways had rubbed off on me. After years of doing his thing he decided to retire and then I took over his weed clientele. Nowadays he was living the straight and narrow life on his savings and I had kept his plug.

A pair of black and white J's were on my feet and I was rocking a True Religion fit of black jeans and a white and black T. My wardrobe was also something that I took pride in as well as my physical appearance. I wouldn't describe myself as a gangster, but I could hold my own in the streets. It wasn't necessary for me to have a crew. The least amount of niggas around me the better.

I had my boys and all, but I didn't depend on them to make money. I made my coins by myself.

At the sound of the doorbell my heart leaped. Elena was something special and we'd been together for a little over a year. I'd met her two years ago at Clark when she was a freshman. She was a good girl, so it took a while for her to agree to let me take her out. Her major was Biology because she wanted to go to medical school to be a Pediatrician.

Not only was my girl smart as hell, but she was also beautiful. The perfect combination of beauty and brains was very important to me. I didn't have to be with the most gorgeous woman in the word, but I was definitely going after the smartest one. It was something about an intelligent, strong minded woman that intrigued me. I didn't go for the hood rat chicks like most of my niggas did.

To be honest Elena was the first chick I'd even thought about getting serious with. Before meeting her I was in my player stage, but I was getting older. Something made me want to settle down with somebody and get serious.

When I opened the door and saw my lady standing there my mouth literally watered with lust.

"C'mon in baby," I said with my cocky, crooked grin intact.

She smiled back at me sexily as she stepped over the threshold. "Hey handsome."

As she kissed the side of my mouth my body shivered.

I closed the door behind her and my eyes were glued to her nice, round ass as she walked off toward the living room to sit down.

Elena was about 5'7 and super thick. I didn't do those skinny broads because I just wasn't interested in playing with a bone. She wore a size 12 and I knew that because I didn't mind buying her clothes. My boo was also a work out buff like me, so her thickness was nice and toned. Damn, I loved her body.

As I stared down at her clear, cocoa brown skin, pretty, big, hazel eyes and nice, full lips, she stared back up at me. She licked those sexy ass lips and I couldn't help but lean over to kiss her deeply. When I pulled away, I brushed a strand of long, dark brown hair behind her ear. It was a weave, but she had naturally thick, shoulder length hair. I understood her reasoning for a sew-in being that Atlanta's weather could be hot and humid.

"What you wanna do tonight?" I was down to go out, but I really just wanted to lay back at the crib.

Hopefully she was on the same page as me.

I sat down beside her and held her warm, soft body close to me.

"I'm kinda tired babe. I had a Calculus exam this morning and you know I just got off work. I don't wanna do shit, but I'll cook us something since I'm hungry." She kissed me before getting up to stretch.

"You know what babe. You had a long day, so how 'bout I go grab us something to eat. What you want?" I pulled my Samsung Galaxy S6 from my pants pocket.

"Hmm, a medium rare sirloin from Outback with a baked potato and broccoli with cheese. Oh, and get some extra sour cream." She was a server at the Cheesecake Factory in Buckhead.

I guess she'd had enough of their food.

She sat back down and got comfy on the sofa as I called the closest Outback Steak House to put in our order. I was told that it would be ready in twenty minutes, so I decided to leave ten minutes after making the call since it would take about a good fifteen minutes to get there. It would take even longer if the traffic was bad.

Elena was already snoring lightly beside me, so I tried not to wake her as I got up to leave. I locked up and headed to my white 2014 Camaro. It was nice and sporty, but didn't call too much attention to a nigga. One thing I didn't like was too much attention.

When my mother passed away I didn't get anything because she never worked, but when my grandmother passed she left me everything in her will. I got my inheritance when I turned eighteen. My mother was an only child and I was Gram's only grandchild. I'd done a good job with my money because I had a nice stash in the bank. My business dealings in the weed game had been lucrative and I could explain my lifestyle with what I had legally got from my grandmother. I missed her and my mom like hell, but life had to go on.

My thoughts were interrupted when this tall, dark skinned nigga yelled out something as he approached me. I'd never seen him before and had no clue what he wanted. If somebody had told him to come to me for some trees I was going to play dumb.

"What's up yo'," he said when we finally closed the distance between us.

What the fuck did he mean? "I'on know you playboy, but I'm good. What's up wit' you?"

He looked me up and down trying to seem intimidating.

"Did I see my girl go inside your spot? I was waiting to see if somebody was gon' come out and shit, but I ain't expect for it to be no nigga," he said.

I frowned up my face because I was confused as hell. "Your what did what and what nigga?"

He just shook his head. "The chick who drives this black Altima right here has been my girl since high school. I came down here from Augusta to surprise her. She claimed she was at work when I called, so I waited for her to get off and followed her here. I thought she was gonna go back to her apartment, but…"

Oh hell to the nah. Elena was his girl? That couldn't be. That nigga must've had my girl mixed up with somebody else.

I chuckled although what he'd said made me feel uncomfortable. "Word my nigga? So, what's her name?"

Saying her name would clear up the bullshit.

"Elena. We've been together for four years."

I shook my head as I headed back toward the door of my townhouse with him on my heels. Although I didn't know that nigga from a can of paint, I was going to let him in because I had to know the truth. There was no damn way. Then I thought about it. She'd always been skeptical about me meeting her family and going home with her and shit. I thought it was because her parents were so strict and she was taking her time letting them know that she was dating somebody.

When I stepped inside she was still asleep so I gave her a rude awakening.

"Elena! Get up! Somebody's here for you!" I yelled not giving a damn about waking her up anymore.

No wonder she was so tired. Juggling two niggas had to be exhausting. There I was trying not to be the player and being faithful to a broad. Where had that shit got my ass other than played? Chicks didn't play me. I must've been slipping.

Her pretty eyes fluttered open and then focused on me. She smiled, but it faded quickly when she spotted dude. Suddenly her eyes were wide open as she sat up.

"Malcolm, what the fuck are you doing here?" She asked as she looked around the room.

"Nah shawty, you ain't dreamin'. This shit's realer than a mufucka," I spoke up.

"What you doin' yo'?" Malcolm asked. "You cheatin' on me wit' this…"

I cut him off. "We been together for over a year man. I ain't have no clue she was fuckin'…well…I meant in a relationship wit' you too."

"Ya'll fuckin'?" He asked her as if he was surprised. What did that nigga expect? "Lena, what the fuck…?"

Elena stood up. "I'm sorry Malcolm, but…I…I've outgrown you and…"

"Why didn't you just say that shit?" He exploded.

That nigga's face was all balled up and he looked like he was about to break down in tears. The wrinkles in his forehead seemed to make him age ten years. I cared about Elena, but I was damn sure not going to take it like that.

All I could do was shake my head. "Ya'll need to handle this shit somewhere else."

Elena's eyes were on me at that point and I could see the regret in them. Still, it didn't matter. It was over. Too bad I didn't get to sample that good good one more time before the truth came out. Shit, I had no clue at all that I was her side nigga.

"Look Keenyn, I didn't mean to…"

I cut her off as I put my hand up. "Nah yo'. Forget that shit. No explanation needed ma. Just leave my spot. You and that nigga. I'm done."

She shook her head as she stared at me. "For real? It's like that?" Tears spilled down her cheeks.

I looked at her like she was crazy and Malcolm did too.

"You gon' do that shit in my face Lena?" He asked as he glared at me like I'd done something to him.

"Don't look at me like you got beef wit' me nigga. I ain't know she was s'posed to be yo' girl, but if you wanna throw hands we can take it there." I had to let him know that those damn looks he kept flashing weren't scaring shit.

Elena put her hand on my chest and I flinched. Dude looked like he wanted to say something, but he didn't. All he did was stare at me like he was mad that I even existed.

"It's no need for all that," Elena said. "I'm sorry…"

"What the fuck ever yo'. Just go."

I pushed her hand away and then turned my back on them. As soon as I did my instinct told me to look behind me. I knew to never turn my back on a rival, but I didn't think that nigga was going to do shit. He was right behind me ready to bust me upside the head with a half full beer bottle that had been on the coffee table. Before he knew what was going on I kicked him in the nuts like a kick boxer and then landed an upper cut to his chin. The bottle hit the hard wood floor and broke into pieces that scattered about. Dude fell against the wall and Elena was crying even harder when she kneeled down to check on him.

"You better get yo' nigga and raise up outta here before shit gets worse." With a scowl on my face, I turned and walked toward the linen closet in the hallway. After grabbing my trusty glock nine I made my way back to see if they were leaving my spot like I'd told them to. If they weren't I was going to make them. I cocked the gun and pointed it in the direction of Elena and Malcolm, who had finally recovered from my assault. Elena's eyes pleaded with me as she chewed nervously on her bottom lip.

Putting her hand out she said innocently, "It doesn't have to come to that. We're going now."

Malcolm's man hood had been depleted, so he didn't even bother to look at me, or say a word. My guess was that nigga wasn't really a fighter. He came off as a square to me right away and so he didn't want to come for me. I guess he had got more than he bargained for. That ass whooping and then the sight of my piece were enough.

I didn't put my gun down. I simply kept it trained on them as she opened the door and let Malcom walk out first. She followed without looking back and then closed the door. I slowly made my way to the door to lock it. The room was quiet as hell as I plopped down on the sofa after cleaning the glass up. I thought about what the fuck had just happened. My girl was cheating on her nigga with me. What the fuck? That shit was crazy. I didn't even have an appetite anymore, so I said fuck Outback.

The only thing was they were blowing my phone up, so I turned my ringer off and smoked a blunt full of Kush. After that I passed out right there on the sofa.

Chapter 2

Keenyn

"Damn nigga, what took you so long to answer the fuckin' phone?" My best friend Dame's familiar voice asked.

"Nigga, you better be glad I looked and saw that mufucka lighting up, 'cause I turned the damn ringer off last night."

"What the fuck man? Why would you do that? I need two of them thangs asap, so make it happen," he said.

I sat up in my bed and thought about the bullshit that had popped off with Elena. That shit could've came to bloodshed, but I wasn't about to catch a murder charge over that broad.

"A'ight nigga. I gotta get straight, so I'll call you after twelve," I said.

"What you mean after twelve nigga? Umm, my phone's been ringin' off the hook all mornin'."

I shook my head. "Look nigga. I can't get it 'till after twelve."

Dame sighed. "You want me to see 'bout somebody else nigga?"

I laughed. "Your threat is empty nigga. We both know better. Ain't nobody else got what I got and you know that shit. It's ten now nigga, damn, two more hours ain't gon' kill yo' ass."

"A'ight man. Hit me up by 12:05. For real." His impatience was clear, and although he was my nigga, I didn't give a fuck.

"Yeah. Already."

We hung up and I noticed that Elena had called and left me a text asking me to call her. NOT! I shook my head and decided to block her number. She was fine and the sex had been good as hell, but it was time for me to move on. My focus wasn't on getting serious with another chick anytime soon. I was young and my plan was to enjoy a multitude of women. Shit, the way I saw it, most women were just as sorry as us niggas.

Elena had proved that shit. She had that good girl act down. I was convinced that I could trust her and that hoe had a man in the stash. It made me wonder how many other niggas she was fucking with. I was glad I'd always wrapped up with her trifling ass. Good thing I hadn't slipped up with that lying broad.

Instead of even giving Elena another thought, I decided to handle my business. I dialed Mendosa's number and waited for him to answer as it rung. After four rings he picked up and spoke in a deep voice that was laced with a slight Jamaican accent. His mother had been born in Jamaica and his father was Spanish, but he never knew him. His parents had met in Jamaica when his father was there on vacation. His mother Rose was a prostitute who would lure the male tourists for sex. His father was originally from Mendoza, Argentina and that was how Mendosa had got his name. It was spelled with an s because that was how the z was pronounced. After his father left Jamaica his mother never saw him again. She named her son Mendosa because that was all she remembered about the stranger who'd impregnated her. When he was five his mother migrated to America. She was killed by her pimp ten years later and Mendosa turned to the streets. That pimp was found dead with a single bullet wound to the head less than a month later. Everybody knew that Mendosa had did it.

"Keys, wah g'wan my nigga?" He'd been in the States for most of his life, so he knew how to disguise his accent.

When we talked he didn't have to. I'd known and looked up to him since I was a kid. He knew that I was loyal, so he looked out for me more than he did the average person. It took a lot for Mendosa to feel anything for anybody and the bond that he had with my father had helped that a lot. My pops, although out of the game, had been loyal to him and so my loyalty lied with Mendosa too.

"Ain't shit man. I need to come check you out."

He let out a grunt in agreement. "Ok. Be at my crib in 'bout an hour."

"A'ight," I agreed before hanging up.

He already knew what it was. Mendosa didn't have to put his hands on his product at all, but he did it for me He knew that I wasn't going to just fuck with anybody. I'd started with him and I only dealt with him. I was the only nigga who did drug business with him at his house. That was simply because my pops used to run a few blocks for him back in the day. Mendosa didn't limit his hustle to weed. He was mostly known on the streets for his cocaine connection. I didn't fuck with that shit. Hell nah. He also had a couple legal businesses under his belt, so sometimes he'd entertain at his home.

After getting dressed in a pair of black basketball shorts and a white wife beater, I headed to my ride. In an instant it felt like somebody was behind me. When I looked back there Elena was standing there.

"What the fuck yo'. For real? I thought I told you that I was done wit' you. Don't be poppin' up over here." I shook my head and proceeded to my whip.

Her hand was on my shoulder. "I didn't mean to hurt you Keenyn."

I laughed mockingly as I turned around to face her. "You think you hurt me? For real? Y'en hurt shit ma. All you hurt was yourself, 'cause I was good to yo' ass. I do what I do, but I treated you better than any nigga you've ever fucked wit'. I know that because I couldn't even tell you had a nigga. Just gone on wit' yo' life Lena. I'm good yo'." When I opened my car door she pushed it closed.

"Can I talk now?" Her eyes were pleading for me to listen to her, but I didn't have time for that shit.

"Umm…" I glanced at my iced out rose gold Gucci watch. "Nah yo'. I got some business to handle."

Her eyes filled with tears, but she looked away to get herself together. "Wow. I really need to talk to you bae. I wish you'd just give me a chance to explain myself."

"It's nothing for you to explain. You got a nigga and you got tired of him. Instead of dumpin' his ass like you should have you kept that nigga 'round just in case shit didn't work out wit' us. I get it. Niggas do it all the time. Even I did it before, but I ain't do it this time. I thought our shit was for real. I see that it wasn't, so just move on. It is what the fuck it is. I can't fuck wit' you like that nomore. I gotta go yo'." I stepped in my car and sat down behind the wheel as she stood there on the sidewalk.

She wiped her eyes with a solemn look on her face.

"So, that's it. You ain't gonna hear me out? Is it that simple? You just gon' leave?" She asked with a look of defeat etched on her face.

She was beautiful, but she wasn't worth it. I drove off without answering her questions. I just wished she was able to let go and move on with her life. In the past I'd never been serious about a chick. Maybe what happened with her was my get back for hurting women. For years I'd dealt with a few chicks at a time and didn't really give a fuck about that shit. Commitment just wasn't my thing. I was getting older and despite my lifestyle, I longed to settle down one day. Finding the right woman to do that shit with was the hard part.

* * *

When I got to the sixteen foot, wrought iron gate with the letters MM, I pressed the button to announce my arrival. Mendosa's housekeeper Ana answered.

"Yes."

"Hi Ana. It's Keys. I'm here to see Mendosa."

Her friendly voice replaced the flat one as she recognized my name. "Oh yes, yes. He not here yet, but I open gate for you."

"Thanks," I said politely as I waited for it to open so I could drive through.

I sent Mendosa a text and he told me to just go ahead and wait for him inside. There was a shiny, candy apple red Range Rover parked in front of the huge estate that I hadn't seen before. I thought I'd seen all of Mendosa's vehicles. Maybe he had got a new toy.

After I rang the doorbell my phone notified me that I had a missed call. It was Elena, but I'd blocked her number. Why didn't she just give the fuck up? When I was done, I was done. Damn. The door swung open and I was face to face with the most gorgeous woman I'd ever laid eyes on in the flesh. She looked like a super star. It was definitely not Mendosa's middle aged, Mexican housekeeper Ana.

I was at a loss for words, but I managed to find my voice. "Umm, hey, I'm Keys and I'm here to see Mendosa. He told me to wait for him…"

"Keenyn, is that you?" She asked with wide eyes that were full of recognition.

All of a sudden I knew who she was. Wow! Who would have ever thought she'd grow up to look like that? Damn! She'd always been pretty, but as a grown woman that shit was on a different level.

"Jasenia?" I couldn't believe it. It had been years since I'd seen her. About ten to be exact.

I stepped inside and grabbed her up into my arms before spinning her around. She was Mendosa's daughter and had also been my best friend when we were kids. Her mother left Mendosa when she was eleven and I was twelve. They ended up moving to Miami and after that I only saw her once. We had managed to stay in touch by email and phone for a few years, but that eventually fizzled away. When I got a Facebook page I searched for her with no luck. I often asked her father about her. He would say that she was studying abroad somewhere like London or Paris during our high school years. Last I heard she was in college down in Florida. I could remember Mendosa recently mentioning that she was about to graduate.

When I planted her feet on the marble floor in the fancy foyer there was still a gorgeous smile on her face. The braces that she'd worn as a child had paid off, because her teeth were perfectly white and straight. Her long hair flowed down to her mid back and was full of bouncy, loose curls. Her flawless make up wasn't caked on, but perfect like it had been done by an artist at Mac. The outfit she wore showed off her curvy, 5'5 frame in high heels and I was enjoying the view. Hmm, I wasn't looking at her like I did when we were kids.

"Wow, look at you." There was a sly look in her eyes that matched her grin. "You've grown into a good looking man...Keys."

"Mmm, shit, look at you..." I shook my head not knowing what adjectives to use to describe her fineness.

Her skin was a smooth, soft mocha tone and her mysterious, slanted eyes were coffee brown. Oh my God, no wonder Mendosa kept her away from me. She was beautiful and I would've definitely tried her by now. Shit.

She led me into the sitting room and my eyes were glued to her round butt as Ana entered with a tray of drinks.

"Hello Mr. Keys. Would you like some lemonade?" There was a pleasant smile on her face.

I smiled back. "Hello Ana, and yes, thank you."

The tart, but sweet, ice cold beverage cooled me down instantly. Ana was right on time. Looking at Jasenia had made me hot as hell. Dayum shawty was bad.

When Ana left the room Jasenia picked up where our conversation had left off. We were sitting together on the sofa and I'd almost forgot that Mendosa would be there soon. I didn't want him to think anything. He'd always been over protective of his daughter.

"Uh, don't you think you should be sitting somewhere else when your pops gets here?" My eyes drifted down to her exposed thigh and I shook my head. "Mmm." I couldn't help it. It just slipped out.

That damn thigh of hers was brown, smooth, firm and thick. I had the urge to reach out and grab it, but I contained myself as I bit down on my bottom lip. The desire that I felt for her was undeniable. I wondered if she felt it too.

"Don't worry about him. It's not like I don't know you." She waved off my statement like it was ridiculous.

"Sen, really?" I referred to her by her childhood nickname. "You know how Mendosa is over you. I heard about how he went down to Florida to visit you and shot some nigga because he was staring at your ass. Besides, you don't know me as a grown man."

She laughed and hit my leg playfully. Her hand lingered there a little longer than I expected. I took another sip of lemonade to distract myself.

"True, but he didn't shoot him. He shot *at* him. He meant to miss," she corrected me.

"What's the difference?" I asked with a shrug of my shoulders. "I ain't tryna get shot or shot at by your crazy old man."

"The difference is that nigga is still breathing and speaking of knowing you as a grown man, I can get to know you." She grabbed my phone. "You're a man, so I know you got some kind of security code on this thing."

I drew the pattern to unlock the phone and passed it back to her. She quickly programmed her number in my contacts under Sen. She passed me the phone back. The look on her face was suddenly serious as she stood up.

As she walked around the room she let out a sigh. "My dad doesn't have any pictures of me in here."

I nodded. "I always noticed that."

"That's because I handle a lot of business in this room. This is where the men I do business with sit. I don't want them salivating over my gorgeous daughter. There are pictures of you all over the living room." Mendosa's rich, commanding voice filled the space.

I wondered how long he'd been there as I looked back at him standing in the doorway.

She walked over to him. "Daddy, I came to surprise you. I have some great news!" Her voice was full of excitement as she hugged him tightly.

"Uh, honey, can we discuss it a little later. I have some business to handle with Keys. I see that you two have gotten reacquainted." There was a look of disapproval on his face. "Why didn't you tell me you were coming over?"

I could tell that he was anxious for her to leave the room so that I could stop ogling her fine ass.

She pouted visibly. "Then it wouldn't have been a surprise. I'll leave you two alone to handle your business." Her eyes drifted to me. "It was nice seeing you again Keys."

"Yeah, you too Sen," I said to her back as she left the room and closed the double doors behind her.

I made sure that my eyes didn't linger on her for too long. Knowing that Mendosa kept a piece on him made me keep my eyes on him.

Suddenly Mendosa smiled. "Don't worry. I ain't gon' shoot you."

I laughed nervously. "I ain't no punk, but my gun's in the car."

He chuckled good-naturedly. "You drinkin' lemonade man? You want something stronger?" He got up to pour some of his expensive Brandy in a tumbler.

"Nah, I'm good." I was about to be riding dirty and I didn't want to be drunk too.

"So, what you tryna get today?" He sipped his drink and sat down in the love seat across from me.

"I need twenty five bricks. Tryna get off them as quickly as possible, but I got back orders, so I need extra."

He nodded. "Good. You know I only keep enough shit here for you."

When he left the room I drained my glass of lemonade wishing that Ana would come into the room with more. Unfortunately she didn't, but Mendosa returned with a black duffle bag that I was sure was filled with compressed bricks of that loud ass green. There was no need for me to even open it to check. I'd always done business with him and his shit was always A one. I passed him the wads of cash that were wrapped in rubber bands and he didn't even bother to count it. He knew that it was all there.

"Thanks Mendosa, but I gotta bounce man."

"No doubt play boy. Tell yo' pops I said what's up. Since he got out the game he don't come around no more."

I stood, put the duffle bag's strap on my shoulder and pounded Mendosa up.

"He's all in love now, living in the country and shit. I'm 'bout to head out there in a lil' while, so I'll tell him."

"A'ight my nigga. Be easy."

"A'ight. Later man."

I left him sitting there sipping on his liquor. As I headed toward the front door I hoped to get the chance to set my eyes on Jasenia again. She wasn't anywhere around and as I opened the door I smiled at the fact that I had her number. Then my smile faded when I thought about Mendosa. He was going to be a hurdle to get over, but something told me that she was worth the risk.

* * *

"You need to get you a trap, or at least get some niggas to do some corner business for you," Dame said as he greeted me at the door of the run down trap spot he sold weed and coke from in College Park.

I looked at that nigga like he was crazy. "You already know how I do man. I'm already riskin' enough just by bein' here wit' how you do shit."

He let out a laugh before his face got serious again. "That was nothin' my nigga. I had to let off some shots yesterday and shit, but it was necessary. That nigga was out of line, so I had to do what I had to do. It was just a shot in the foot anyway. He'll live."

I shook my head at my pecan brown skinned homeboy with the golden brown eyes and shoulder length locks. He was about 5'10 and muscular as hell. He was the wild one and I was more laid back. I guess you could say that we were polar opposites. That nigga liked trouble and looked for it as much as possible. Me on the other hand, I was more careful and low key about how I did shit.

"Y'en have to shoot Ray in his foot man. I'm sure it wasn't that damn serious. You just get a kick out of fuckin' wit' people."

He'd closed and locked the door behind me so that we could complete our transaction.

"That mufucka was tryna holla at one of my bitches. I'on play that shit. A nigga ain't fuckin' wit' not one of my hoes unless I let him. I didn't let him, so he got shot in the damn foot," Dame explained with a matter of fact look on his face.

"Nigga, you be on one for real. Zero to a hundred real damn quick. You know you don't give a fuck about them broads you be fuckin wit'."

He passed me the money before I removed the two bricks from the waist of my jeans.

"You right my nigga, but it's the principle. If I'm dickin' a hoe down a nigga gotta wait 'till I'm finished wit' her. I own each and every pussy I fuck and until I'm done ain't no other nigga gon' fuck."

That nigga was as serious as he could be and I could only shake my head.

"You gotta be kiddin' me man. You really think that hoe Sasha is only fuckin' you and she always been a hoe. Shit, I remember when that hoe was tryna fuck me. I couldn't do it though. Her pussy smelled like decayed meat. I hope you ain't fuckin' that raw nigga." I shook my head with a frown on my face as I remembered that shit.

"That hoe got some good head. That's all."

I didn't say a word. Dame was the type of nigga who'd fuck if the bitch was a freak and that bitch Sasha was a certified freak. He didn't give a fuck what she smelled like. Being a picky nigga was my thing. If the pussy smelled suspect, I wasn't trying to go up in it. Shit, condoms broke every damn day and I wasn't getting caught up with no babies, or no life threatening disease.

"Do you man. I'm dirty as hell, so I gotta head out and put that shit up."

Dame pounded me up. "A'ight. Thanks for comin' through man. Shit's been dry 'round here, so you might be able to get some new clientele. I'll hit you up later 'bout that though."

"Already," I said before heading out to my car.

It was almost two o' clock and I knew that my pops would be at the spot. I just had to make sure before I made that long ride.

"Sup youngun'?"

"Not much pops. Just got right and need to make a drop off."

"A'ight. I'll be here."

"Cool. Mendosa asked about you. He said he don't see you now that you out the game and shit."

"That's the whole point." He chuckled. "I'm out, so what I need to see him for."

I laughed, but my mind was on Jasenia. After I got that shit off me I was going to call and see what she had going on for the night.

Chapter 3

Jasenia

"So, what's the news you got for me baby girl?"
My father asked as he sat down beside me on the sofa.
There was a twinkle in his eye that was reserved for only
me.

I'd made my way back to the sitting room after
Keenyn was long gone, but my father wasn't there.
Instead of leaving I decided to wait for him. Besides, I'd
told him that I had something to tell him. Ana had said
that he was in his study and would be out soon. Well, it
was thirty minutes later and I guess he was finally ready
to listen to me.

My father was an intimidating man and that
wasn't just because he'd given me life. He had a
commanding presence and a voice that was very deep,
loud and boisterous. He stood about 6'4 with dark,
mahogany toned skin. His dark eyes resembled mine, but
his were more brooding and hid behind naturally long
lashes. I had nice lashes as well, but of course I liked to
get extensions like most women. Not only was he tall, but
my father also had a large, broad chest as well as long,
muscular legs. At the age of 40 he was in the best shape
of his life.

"Well," I let out a nervous sigh before forcing a
smile on my face. "I'm moving back here."

There was a blank stare on my father's face and I
could've sworn I heard crickets chirping. "Daddy, say
something."

He blinked and then shook his head. "What about school?"

"I'm practically done. All I need is one more class that wasn't offered in the spring and I'm taking that online so I can march in December. C'mon daddy, don't look like that. I want to spend more time with you. I mean, over the years we haven't spent that much time together."

He knew that I was right and I could tell by how his face seemed to soften. "You sure about this? What does Melissa think?"

I shrugged my shoulders indifferently. "I mean, it really doesn't matter what she thinks. I'm an adult and I thought about it. I'm sure."

He pulled me into his arms for a tight hug. "What about grad school?"

I rolled my eyes glad that he couldn't see because I was enveloped in his strong arms. "I'm working on that. Can I graduate first?"

He laughed. "I'm proud of you Sen."

He told me those words often, but at that moment they made my heart drop.

"Thank you daddy," I said softly as I ignored that voice in my head that screamed for me to tell him the truth.

Finally, he released me from his tight embrace. "So, are you stayin' here? Do you have a place already? I know how your mother is. I'm sure she set you up with something without lettin' me know. Melissa got some shit wit' her ass." He shook his head. "Uh, if so I'd like to know what neighborhood my little girl will be livin' in." He lit up one of his Cuban cigars and sat back with his drink in hand.

I was surprised that he wasn't sitting in his favorite dark brown, butter leather recliner. It was apparent that he wanted to sit close to me. We hadn't really bonded in a while, so it was nice to spend some quality time with him. The only thing was, my father could see right through me. I felt like he was reaching and probing for information. For some reason he could sense something. I had to do a better job of masking the truth from him.

"You know your ex-wife." I let out a slight chuckle hoping that bringing up my mother would distract him from me. "She got me an apartment in Midtown, so don't worry. It's a safe area. I promise."

His brow lifted in surprise and his eyes bore into my soul. I had to look away.

"So, you've already moved in? When?"

I cleared my throat. "The movers dropped everything off before I got here yesterday."

He didn't say anything for a while and then said in a fatherly tone, "I'll be there to check it out tomorrow."

I knew not to argue. When Mendosa said something it was law.

"Can you just call me before you come?" I asked meekly as I looked down at my perfectly manicured fingers nails.

No matter how old I was, my father made me feel like that. I was his only child, so he spent all of his time and attention on shaping me into the ideal daughter. He wanted me to take a different path than him and my mother. It was too bad that I'd failed him. So many things had gone down that I hadn't planned for. My mind and heart weren't always in the right place. That was probably because I'd been spoiled all of my life. At that point, when it came to money, I really didn't give a fuck what I had to do, or who I had to hurt to get it. Well, I did have a few limits. Because of my pops I was used to a certain lifestyle and I wanted more and more.

See, I was addicted to doing fucked up shit. For some reason I was just drawn to making the wrong decisions. Maybe that was because of what I knew about my parents. They were both goons. Neither of them had ever lived a legal lifestyle, so why did they want to push that shit on me?

Yeah, I was in college majoring in Biochemistry. I wanted to work in a pharmaceutical lab and do research for curing diseases such as Cancer, Sickle Cell, Diabetes and AIDS. However, even with that dream, there were other things that I made a priority first. Now that I looked at it, my decisions had blown up in my face. Shit, I couldn't tell my dad the whole truth. Even my mother and Nadia didn't know everything. Nobody knew; well expect for me, God and my demons.

My father shifted in his seat and then took a long, deliberate drag from his cigar. There was a contemplative expression on his face and then he seemed to relax. He didn't speak until after he exhaled the smoke.

"Well, you're an adult now, so I guess I can give you that respect."

I was surprised, but I tried to play it off as I kissed his cheek lovingly.

"Thanks daddy."

"Just make sure you don't have no knuckle head ass nigga over there." His face was stern and his glare was direct.

I nodded obediently. "I won't."

He finally smiled. "Good, so do you need any money or anything? I can put something in your account in the morning."

My face lit up. "Thanks dad. You know this move wiped me out."

He chuckled. "All I need for you to do is get your degree, stay out of trouble and not get pregnant. That's all your daddy can ask for. I don't want you throwin' your future away for one of them no good ass niggas out there."

"Don't worry about that. I got my head on straight. I promise." My heart thumped erratically against my rib cage. If he was giving me a lie detector test I'd be failing miserably.

It was a good thing I was a good actress, because my face and body language didn't give me away.

He nodded and then let out a sigh of relief.

"Good, 'cause I'd hate to kill a nigga."

That made my heart drop. My father was relentless when it came to his grind and me. His money and his daughter were all that he really gave a shit about. That was why I couldn't really be myself around him. Out of fear of him being disappointed or somebody getting murdered, I kept a lot of things a secret from him. As I stared into my father's eyes I realized that no matter how close we were, neither of us *really* knew the other.

* * *

"Girl, that mufucka's so damn fine…oh my God," I filled my best friend Nadia in as I drove back to my new spot.

Yeah, when I talked to my closest friend I didn't sound college educated at all. Despite the education that I'd obtained and the life that my parents had afforded me, I still had that street edge. That was thanks to my parents because they'd both come from the hood.

Nadia lived in Miami and I missed her like crazy. I didn't really fuck with any chicks like that in Atlanta. Honestly I didn't have many female friends in Florida either. I only dealt with women other than Nadia when it came to making some funds and most times that didn't end well. That alone gave me that fuck bitches attitude.

Nadia had been my A one since I first moved to Miami, so I was loyal to her and she was loyal to me.

"Hmm, what about Trell?" She asked throwing me off my square with that question.

My stomach churned and suddenly I felt queasy. I was starting to get tired of my boyfriend of only six months already. It was like he had changed over such a short period of time and it wasn't for the better. I was surprised to see that he didn't give a fuck about who my father was. The bad thing about that was the fact that Trell knew his reputation. My pops would end a nigga's life for me and that was just the way it was. Still, Trell didn't care and he knew that I was in a bad spot.

"Fuck him. That nigga's not who I thought he was. You'd think since we practically grew up together that he'd treat me with at least an ounce of respect."

My bestie didn't say anything for a while. "You left Atlanta when you were eleven Jasenia. You don't know him anymore."

That reminded me of what Keenyn had said earlier. I had been telling Nadia all about our little reunion before she brought Trell up. Yeah, a decade could make a drastic difference in a person, but something told me that Keenyn hadn't changed. I was certain that he was still the same cool, laid back person that I'd known when I was a little girl. Trell on the other hand was still the same rude, mischievous boy from my childhood. I thought he'd grown up, but he hadn't. Not one bit. Now I understood why my father never wanted me around him when I was younger.

Even now that I was grown he still talked about how much he didn't respect Trell, who was now a ruthless, dope boy.

Damn, a bitch like me just loved those damn street niggas. A thug was just, mmm, so appealing to me. Maybe it was because the first man that I'd ever loved was a thug. My father was my hero and I longed for a man like him. True, I was a very intelligent, refined young lady. I'd gone to boarding school in London and studied abroad during the summers in France and even South Africa. It was a worldly experience that had taught me a lot about life.

I was supposed to graduate from college in the winter and my major in Biochemistry was not the easiest. Regardless of that, I still loved those bad boys. I'd dated college guys, and even professional men who made six or seven figures, but they were all boring as hell. Not only that, but college guys couldn't afford me. My father had set a standard that they just couldn't compete with. Although a professional man could afford me, he just couldn't hold my interest for too long. The shit was frustrating as hell, because it was clear that a bad boy was nothing but a clear route to jail or the grave.

I sighed. "You're right DiDi. It's like…I'on know. He just seems so…aggressive lately and I think he's cheating on me. It hasn't even been a year yet and I'm feeling like this already. I moved here to be with him…" My thoughts drifted because that wasn't the only reason that I'd moved to Atlanta. Of course I'd told my father that I was there to spend more time with him as well, but there was so much more to the story.

Not only did I suspect that Trell was cheating on me, but he was becoming more and more intolerable by the day. For some odd reason I still wanted to work it out with him. Then another part of me just wanted to let it go. Something told me that despite who my father was, shit wasn't going to be that easy when it came to Trell.

"Don't be nobody's fool boo. The Sen that I know won't allow any nigga to play her. Don't switch up on me, or I'm gonna have to disown your ass."

We both laughed.

"You're right. I'm gonna have to put my foot down with his ass and remind him of what the fuck he got. I ain't some low budget, no class having ass hoe runnin' 'round this bitch. Fuck that shit. I won't allow him to treat me like I'm some thot. I'm far from that. I'm almost done with my degree, I push a Range, got my own place and all types of shit in my walk in closet. He must not know 'bout *this bitch*. Shit. Those hoes he been fuckin' must have their hands out and shit, because I don't need him. Mendosa's my father and I ain't gotta want for a muthafuckin' thing. Hmm." I was all out of breath.

Nadia's cackle of a laugh was contagious and even with the bullshit going on in my life, I couldn't help but join in. "Damn bitch. Your ass done went off and shit."

"For real. Shit. I'm gonna call him and tell him to come over so we can talk. I have to get this shit off my chest before I do something crazy with all of these fucked up ass emotions girl."

"I feel you boo. Just be careful, because from what you've told me he's a beer short of a six pack. Don't make me have to call my goons and make a trip up there. You know I will bitch."

That made me smile because my boo was a ride or die all day every day. "I know. Let me call that fool. I'll hit you up tomorrow. Okay."

"Okay," she agreed. "Love you chica."

"And I love you back. Muah!"

We hung up and I decided to wait and call Trell when I got home. In a way I was hoping that Keenyn would call me. Damn, if only I'd ran into him that night instead of Trell.

* * *

Instead of calling Trell right away, I decided to strip down and take a nice, long, hot shower. Water always seemed to relax me and I needed to wind down before we talked. At the moment I needed to get my thoughts together. Something told me that it wasn't going to be easy to get through to him.

My choice to move to Atlanta was only going to prove to be hazardous if we stayed together, but with the situation that I'd gotten into, it was my only choice. Although he didn't know what was going on, I had to be closer to my father. I needed his protection just in case some crazy shit that I'd done came back to haunt me like a ghost.

The sensual aroma of my Gucci Guilty body wash filled the confines of the bathroom as steam covered the glass door of the shower. Brown and beige Italian Marble tiles surrounded me as the water's pressure beat down on my weary body. Instead of clearing my mind, the shower only seemed to make me think more.

Thoughts of Trell were swimming around in my mental despite the ritual that usually relaxed me. I sighed as the hot tears fell down my cheeks, mixing with the stream of water that spewed from the double shower head. It was seven months ago when I ran into Trell at a hot spot in downtown Miami.

"Sen, that you?" A deep, masculine voice called out behind me when I was on my way out.

I spun around in my six inch stiletto heels and was face to face with so much fineness that I almost lost my balance. His face didn't register in my memory, which caused me to ask the next question.

"Who the fuck are you?" My first thought was to be defensive because I didn't know what that nigga was up to. Did he know who my father was? Was he there to gun me down in front of a packed ass club? I knew that anything could happen with the lifestyle that my father lived and I was prepared.

He grinned, flashing one sexy dimple and an iced out grill. I wasn't really feeling the grill, but I was feeling his features and his build. He was about 6'2, with flawless, cocoa brown skin that was covered in neatly trimmed facial hair. I mean, his side burns, beard and moustache were on point. It was obvious that he was a dope boy and I wondered what hot whip in the parking lot belonged to him.

"Damn, you a feisty one. You don't know who I am shawty?" His forehead creased as he pushed his eyebrows together, feigning surprise.

His accent sounded like he was from ATL, but I hadn't really spent much time there since I was a kid. My dad would often come to Miami to visit me. He wanted to keep me and his lifestyle separate after him and my mother's divorce. Honestly, I liked Miami better and after spending so much time out of the States, I was glad to be studying at home.

"Am I supposed to know you or something?" My hands were on my hips and I threw mad attitude as I narrowed my eyes into slits. How else would he know my name?

That sexy ass grin invaded his handsome face again. My eyes were on his muscular arms and wide chest. His waist was slim and I could only imagine what he was packing in those dark blue jeans. I could tell that he'd just pulled the tags off. Even his J's were crisp like they'd just been taken out of the box.

"Wow, you can't be for real right now." His smile was gone and he looked genuinely disappointed that I didn't recognize him.

Then I thought about that time last year, when I visited my father for New Years. Nadia had gone with me and of course we partied like two wild, ratchet ass bitches. We both got pissy drunk and I woke up in a hotel suite at the W with some strange nigga. I woke up the next morning butt naked and he was sprawled next to me. Immediately I thought about my dad. I couldn't be that reckless because of him.

When I looked in the trash can and saw the Magnum wrapper I felt relieved. At least he'd used protection. All I could do was hope he'd kept it on because I didn't remember shit. As I got dressed and stumbled out of the bedroom I ran into Nadia who was walking out of another bedroom. I hadn't been to ATL since. Was he that nigga? I honestly could not remember his face at all.

"Uh, I'm for real and if you don't tell me who you are by the time the valet pulls my Range up, it won't matter. I got shit to do," I snapped.

The sexy stranger glanced down at his platinum Rolex and shook his head. "What the hell you gotta do at 3 am other than go get some breakfast wit' me?"

I couldn't help but smile sexily at that. "Just go ahead and tell me how you know my name, and I might."

"I'm Trell. We used to go to school together back in Atlanta. C'mon shawty, we played in the sandbox together and shit," he said with that smile on his face again.

"How the hell did you recognize me in a dark ass club after ten years?" I asked suddenly giving him a suspicious look.

Honestly, I still didn't remember him.

"Nah shawty, I remember when you came down to visit your pops a while back. I was at Lenox Mall wit' my nigga Jus and he pointed yo' fine ass out talkin' 'bout you Mendosa's daughter. I never stopped thinkin' 'bout yo' fine ass, so I can't help but remember you. It just so happened that I came down here wit' a couple of my niggas. I saw you a few times in the club and I was wondering if it was you. Once we got out here where it's some light, I knew it was. Like I said, I'd never forget a face…or a body like yours. Real talk."

That long ass speech had my attention, but I had to give my ticket to the valet and move on.

"How long will you be here?" I asked as I unlocked my car door with the remote key.

"A few more days," he said vaguely as his eyes scanned my face and then dropped to the cleavage that was oozing out of my low cut top.

"It's too soon for me to go to breakfast with you. Maybe we'll get together before you leave. What's your number?" I was playing it safe because I'd made so many bad decisions about men in the past. Repeating history over and over again was not my thing.

As he recited each digit I punched it into my phone and then saved his name as Trell ATL. Once I was

behind the wheel heading away from the club, I
remembered exactly who he was. His name was Latrell
Robertson and we had gone to elementary and middle
school together. Of course he looked different after ten
years and he went by the nickname Rocky back then. A
smile spread across my face, but soon faded. I could
remember my father telling me how much he couldn't
stand Trell when we were kids.

When I thought about it, I could kind of
understand why. Trell wasn't as polite and respectful as
Keenyn. He loved to fight and cussed like a sailor. I
could remember when Trell came to my tenth birthday
party and my pops called his father to tell him to come
get him. That fool was wreaking havoc like a human
version of the Tasmanian Devil. Not only was he starting
fights with all of the kids, including the girls, but he went
off and broke a window just because he couldn't break
the pinata.

Lost in my thoughts, I turned the water off and
grabbed a towel as I stepped out of the shower. Without
even drying off, I walked into my bedroom and called
Trell.

"Shawty…sup ma?"

I rolled my eyes starting to resent the small things
that I liked about him at first. He had swag and he was a
brash, shit talking ass nigga. That had initially turned me
on, but now I was wondering if I should've took his
behavior as a kid as a warning sign. I liked dope boys
who made lots of money and did all types of foul shit in
the streets, but I didn't like being mistreated. One thing I

didn't take was a man's abuse. With a father like Mendosa, I didn't have to.

"Nothing. I just got out of the shower," I said before getting straight to the point. "We need to talk."

"Y'en wait for yo' man shawty? Damn, that's fucked up, but it's cool. I'm pullin' up now, so I guess I'm right in time for that talk huh?" His voice proved his disinterest.

I was sure that he didn't take what I said seriously. Trell tended to be shallow as hell and didn't have a deep bone in his body. Not only did that nigga do all types of illegal shit, but he didn't give a fuck who he hurt while doing it. As long as he got his paper, he was good. It wasn't just about making money either. He enjoyed everything that came with his lifestyle, especially murder.

"Why didn't you call me first?" I hated that pop up bullshit.

"I did call you ma. Y'en answer. You was in the shower remember? Come open the door yo'."

I decided to not even argue about it since we needed to talk anyway. As I made my way to the door I let out a deep sigh not knowing exactly how our conversation was going to turn out.

Chapter 4

Keenyn

"What's up son?" My pops pounded me up with a smile on his face.

His girlfriend Kelly was eight years younger than him and looked at least my age. She glanced up at me with light brown eyes.

"Hey Keenyn," she called out with a smile on her caramel complexioned face.

There was a slight gap between her teeth that was actually kind of sexy to me. I hated to look at my father's woman, but she was thick to death. I mean, pops wasn't a bad looking man either, so I could see it. The thing was, Kelly was just too damn fine. She ran her fingers through her short, pixie style haircut and stood up. I had to look away because she was rocking a short ass pair of shorts and a low cut shirt.

"I'm gonna go upstairs and let ya'll have your time." She licked her lips flirtatiously before leaving the room.

"Mmm mmm mmm," my pops said as he shook his head.

I could imagine what was on his mind as I sat down on the sofa. He sat down beside me.

"So, you got some work to drop off huh? That's the only time you come over here." He smiled despite what he'd just said.

"Stop playin' old man. You the one that's always booed up and shit."

He laughed and took a swig from a Bud Light bottle. "You see how fine she is. Shit, you'd be booed up too."

I nodded in agreement and thought about Sen. If I had a chick who looked like her, I'd be booed up too. "Yeah, you right."

"You do have a lil' girlfriend though right? She's cute. What's her name…?"

"Elena and nah, we broke up." I didn't go into it.

"Why?" His smile faded. "You want a beer."

"She had a man back home and yeah, a beer would be on time right now."

"Damn and go get it yourself. You know where the refrigerator is."

I smirked at him and shook my head before heading to the kitchen. After grabbing a beer I walked back into the sitting area. The television was on ESPN and Sports Center was on. I wanted to hear what was going on, but my pops had the TV on mute. That let me know that he wanted to talk about something. Usually he'd have the volume on full blast and I'd be on the back burner.

"So, what's goin' on old man?" I asked when I sat down.

"Old man? Nigga please. I'd fold yo' ass up in here and then you'll see just how old I am." There was a serious look on his face, but I knew better. He didn't really want to try me.

True, back in the days he did do business with Mendosa and sold marijuana and cocaine. My pops was infamous for not taking no shit and his reputation always surpassed him, retired or not. He had pulled out of the illegal lifestyle almost five years ago, but he let me keep my work in the shed behind his two story brick house. There were a few locks on the shed and he lived in a pretty good area that was secluded, so I didn't really worry. Besides, nobody knew what was in there anyway.

"Not much. I just..." He cleared his throat. "I was thinkin' of gettin' back in the game."

I was confused. "Why?"

He shrugged his shoulders before guzzling the rest of his beer. "I just miss it. Besides, it wouldn't hurt to get a lil' extra dough."

I thought about that. That younger bitch he was fucking with must've been high maintenance as hell.

"Is it Kelly?"

Letting out a sigh, he scratched his head and then said, "Kinda. I mean, I don't wanna have to compete with these young cats. I got a lil' money, but...she got expensive taste. I love her Keys."

"I know you do pops, but damn, is she worth it? You got out and I thought you were good..."

"I *am good,* but not enough."

I thought about it. Had messing around with Kelly put him in a bad spot financially? Instead of asking I just offered him some advice instead.

"Do what you feel you gotta do old man. I got your back. Just think about it first. Okay."

He shook my hand. "Okay. Thanks son."

We talked a little longer before I decided to pull my car around back and load the shed up. Once I was done I said my goodbyes to my pops and got in my car. I was headed home and thought about calling Jasenia, but before I could my phone started ringing.

When I looked down at the screen I noticed that it was Dame.

"Sup man?"

"My nigga, what you got goin' on?"

I could already tell that something was up with his slick ass and I wasn't in the mood for it. Dame had been my best friend since we were four years old. On the first day of Pre K we just seemed to click like brothers. We'd been close as hell ever since. Back then this nigga named Trell was part of our crew too and then we included JJ. Over the years we'd fallen out with Trell and he had his own crew of niggas who had ambitions of running the East Side, but Mendosa had a strong hold on Atlanta period.

Dame's crew ran a trap and some blocks on the West Side and although he and Trell had been close until some bullshit that had gone down in high school, they beefed constantly in the streets. I personally didn't believe in having a crew to make money. I sold potent ass weed to a small, reliable clientele and didn't believe in all of that flossing and showing off. I liked nice shit though, but I knew how to stay under the radar and be seen when I wanted to be.

"What's goin' on now nigga?" I had my eyes on the scene because I'd left my Bluetooth at the crib. I didn't want the cops to fuck with me because I was talking on the phone. Dekalb County police were some greedy ass mufuckas and they couldn't wait to hem up a young, black man. The thing was, I was only a few classes away from a Criminal Justice degree and I knew the law as well as my rights. However, I had no clue what I was going to do with that shit. Honestly, I only wanted the education and not necessarily an honest job. I was used to being a hustler and so I was comfortable with my hustle.

"Nothin' man." He laughed. "That nigga JJ was just here askin' me to give him a OZ 'til the end of the week."

I shook my head. "I just fronted that nigga a eighth yesterday. What the fuck?"

"I'on know man, but that nigga's fallin' off and shit."

I didn't say anything because I knew that his call had to be about something else other than JJ's begging ass. Something told me that he was in some shit and he needed my cool as a cucumber ass to defuse it.

"Yeah, but what's really up nigga? Get to the fuckin' point."

Dame got a little weed from me here and there to get off of, but he really fucked with coke. He got that pure, uncut shit from Mendosa of course. He had tried to pull me into the coke game with him time and time again, but it was a no go. I'd seen firsthand what the lifestyle had done to my pops and decided to stick with weed. It was dangerous too, but the people I sold to didn't seem as volatile as those ruthless niggas in the coke game. Mo' money, mo' problems like Biggie had said. Yeah, Mendosa and my pops had me on that old school music.

"Shit, straight up man, Come by my crib." Dame's voice sounded funny and I was wondering what he wanted me to meet him at his crib for.

We'd already done business for the day and I wasn't really in the mood to hang out.

"Nah nigga, I'm goin' home. I ain't in the mood to be fuckin' wit' yo' crazy ass." Whenever I went out with that nigga it was a fight or a shootout.

I didn't like to bring attention to myself, so getting into disputes and shit wasn't really my thing. A nigga like me could hold my own, but I really didn't like to be put in the position to pull a trigger. Arguing wasn't my thing, but I didn't mind throwing some hands. The only thing about that was the fact that niggas my age didn't believe in fighting. They always wanted to pull out a strap, so I made sure that I had mine at all times. So, my nine was in the arm rest waiting for a nigga to test me. That was why it was best for me to just make my money and lay low.

"What you mean man? It ain't nothing like that. I ain't in the mood to get in no shit either. Look, you my right hand my nigga. We ain't got fucked up and just chopped it up in a while. Just come through for a lil' minute. I got a proposition for you." His voice was full of the malice that I knew flowed through his veins.

All of my friends that I'd grown up with were different from me. They were calculating and self-serving. I often wondered what they would or wouldn't do for a come up. JJ and Dame were the only niggas I really fucked with now and my loyalty to them was never in question. Mendosa and my pops were the only real family that I had and my loyalty lied with them as well. Still, you never knew what kind of hate and contempt another nigga was holding on to.

"A'ight. I'm on my way," I said reluctantly.

Shit, I needed to chill and smoke a blunt or two anyway.

* * *

About forty five minutes later I was pulling up in Dame's driveway behind a dark blue Impala. Something told me that it was one of his bitches. That nigga had two baby mamas and at least three or four chicks he was fucking on a regular. That didn't even include the random bitches he was dicking down. I was surprised that nigga's dick hadn't fell off yet, because he didn't have no standards.

That nigga loved strippers and freaky ass thots who'd do any and everything for a few dollars. He'd buy those hoes knock off purses and shoes and they'd be his forever. All he had to do was give them some dick and tell them all of the bullshit they wanted to hear. Then, like Dr. Jekyll and Mr. Hyde, that nigga'll switch up on their asses. He'd beat on them and like fools they'd stick around.

I'd learned my lesson about playing captain save a hoe for them. About a year and a half ago he was beating up on some chick and I tried to get him to stop. That hoe told me that it was none of my business and I should leave that shit alone because she loved her man. She ain't have to tell me twice. I was at home less than twenty minutes later. The next day Dame called me talking about how he'd choked that bitch out. After that she came back for more. Next thing I knew, she was baby mama number two.

For some reason women just flocked to Dame. I didn't understand that shit at all. Maybe it was his money, but he was really a stingy nigga. Why did women give a fuck about a man's whip, or his crib if he didn't give them shit? It was like so what, you got a key to the crib and a key to one of his rides. He could take that shit away at any time. When a woman owned the key to a nigga's heart, then she was doing something.

That was why I didn't do dumb broads. I was seeking something real. My soul yearned for a woman who had standards and knew that she deserved a man like me and not an asshole like my boy Dame. Yet and still, he pulled way more chicks than me. Not that I wasn't good looking. I guess I just wasn't all flossy and aggressive like my best friend. I was the exact opposite. A nigga like me didn't believe in beating on no female.

Deep down inside, I was a hopeless romantic who was looking for a good woman to fill that empty hole; a void that I'd felt for most of my life. I needed a woman who was looking for longevity and not how long my pockets and dick were. I was a good dude, but women didn't want good dudes. They always fell for the wrong niggas and then wondered why they felt so unfulfilled and disrespected.

Before I could even make it to the steps of Dame's house the door opened and he had some chick hemmed up by the collar of her shirt. All I could do was walk faster and try to keep him from catching a charge like always.

"What's goin' on nigga?" I asked him. "I just talked to your ass."

He gave me a stern look like he was telling me to mind my own business and then focused back on the broad who I'd never seen before. "Bitch, how you gon' pop up over here after I done told yo' hoe ass! Don't play them games wit' me! My baby mama was 'bout to cut you and you don't wanna know what I'm gon' do to yo' trick ass!"

She was pretty as fuck with natural, bouncy, light brown curls, and soft, copper brown eyes. Not only was her facial features on point, but lil' mama was thick and my eyes were on her in black tights and a gray, work out shirt. She had on sneakers, so I figured she'd came to fight. There was a scratch under her left eye, so I figured it had already gone down.

"Shit," I said under my breath.

Dame's baby mama Arica showed up at the door with a busted lip, but that time instead of a knife, she had a .45 in her hand.

"I'm so fuckin' sick of yo' bitches Dame!" Tears were streaming down her cheeks and my heart started to beat a mile a minute.

Suddenly she pointed the gun at him and it seemed like everything was happening in slow motion.

"Put the gun down Arica," I said in a soothing voice.

She looked at me, but her eyes were empty. She was the first baby mama; the one he'd been with him since high school.

"Keys?" She said my name like it was a question as her bottom lip quivered. "What you doing here?"

There was a slight smile on her face when she spotted me and I was hoping that I'd distracted her.

"Put the gun down ma. It ain't worth it. Think about DJ." I figured that mentioning their son would give her some clarity about the situation.

She laughed and that shit not only sounded evil, but it was like she was really genuinely amused.

"I'm so tired of your boy's bullshit Keys." She wiped her eyes with her free hand. "All I do is ride for his ass and all his sorry, trifling ass can do is cheat on me and make babies and shit!"

POW! POW!

Arica let off a couple rounds in the air after she stepped out on the porch.

"Get the fuck outta here bitch, 'fore I shoot yo' triflin' ass!"

The chick skedaddled to the car that I'd parked behind and I rushed to go move my ride. I was on the street and she was pulling out of the driveway when Arica started shooting again.

POW! POW! POW!

She was aiming at old girl's tires because she wanted to stop her escape. I had counted five shots so far. That .45 had a few more rounds left and I hoped she'd stop shooting before somebody really got hurt. It was a good thing the chick got away and Dame had finally talked Arica into giving him the gun.

"I should've shot yo' ass!" She yelled at him. "I just wanted to get that bitch, 'cause I can always get you later nigga!"

I gave Dame a look and shook my head. It wasn't out of sympathy. Honestly, it was that "I told you so" look. He'd already been through enough drama and bullshit with Arica and I couldn't understand why she stayed with him. Damian Jr. didn't deserve to see his parents fighting twenty four seven. He was four years old, but he knew what was going on. His daughter Damisha was four months old and of course her mother, baby mama number two Deliah, was going through it too.

I stepped into the house and followed my best friend to the basement. Arica had gone upstairs to keep fuming I guess. All I knew was, I didn't want to be in that nigga's position. I'd had my situation with Elena, but it was nothing like that.

"Wow man, that shit could've ended bad as fuck. Somebody might report them gun shots."

Dame shook his head and lit a blunt that was in the ashtray. "I know nigga. You ain't gotta tell me. Let that bitch handle that."

I shook my head at his reference to Arica as a bitch. "That chick was bad as hell though. Who the fuck was that?"

Don't get me wrong, Arica was bad too. She was about 5'3, nice curvy shape, with light brown skin, innocent, honey colored eyes, thick lips and deep ass dimples. She usually wore sew-ins or braids, but she had her own hair. Not only was she fine, but she was actually classy and smart. She was always a good student and was going to earn her nursing degree in a few months. Dame wasn't worth her losing all of that. Her first priority should've been her son.

"That was Denise. She a chick I met at the gas station a month or so ago. That hoe don't mean shit to me. We fucked a few times and when I stopped callin' her she decided to start stalkin' my ass. Of course she found out where the trap's at, so she followed me here from there and shit." He took a few pulls of the good smelling bud and passed it to me.

I took it gratefully and took one long pull after another.

He shrugged his shoulders and continued. "I'm sick and tired of these hoes man. I'm good to them and..."

I tuned that bi-polar ass sounding nigga out. He wasn't good to anybody, not even himself. Then I stopped and thought about it. Who was I to talk? I didn't sell coke or crack, but I was still living up to white America's stereo-type of the black man by selling weed. I didn't gang bang or do drive bys, but I still toted a glock nine. Not only did I carry that shit, but I wasn't afraid to use it. Did that make me a menace to society too? In my eyes I was just armed to defend myself, not to end lives for no reason at all.

But still, I'd end a life for a reason.

"Dame, man, seriously, you need to slow the fuck down. Arica's a good girl and she's okay wit' you messin' around with Deliah. Don't fuck up what you got. You gon' get yourself or somebody else killed and you got kids to think about."

He nodded. "You're right man. My sister wives both fine as shit. I should be satisfied, but I ain't though. I love new pussy man."

All I could do was sit back and try to get comfy on the sofa. Something told me not to get too damn comfortable though. A woman scorned could make a weapon out of anything. As we got high all I could think about was Arica coming downstairs to kill Dame because she was fed up. What if she forgot all about our own friendship and killed me too because she thought I was enabling his cheating ways.

After the blunt was gone I realized that it was too damn quiet. What if Arica was plotting for real? I stood up and decided to get my ass up out of there. Dame was my boy and shit, but he'd got himself in that fucked up ass situation. I'd filled him in on what had gone down with Elena and I couldn't believe that he called himself warning me.

"You better watch out for that hoe and her nigga," he advised me.

I smirked at him. "Yeah nigga, whatever. You the one who need to watch out."

"Oh yeah." There was a thoughtful look on his face. "I got some shit to talk to you about my nigga. What happened earlier threw me off."

I agreed with a nod. "Oh yeah, that proposition that you mentioned. That shit threw us both off."

Dame's eyes drifted over to the sofa. "Sit down nigga. Let's talk."

The skeptical side of me wanted to get the hell up out of there, but he was my boy. "A'ight." I sat down. "This shit better be good man."

Chapter 5

Jasenia

That ignorant ass nigga wasn't trying to hear anything that I was trying to tell him. All he wanted to do was get his damn dick sucked. Well, we were not on the same fucking page.

"Go ahead Trell," I pushed him away. He grabbed me around my waist and pulled me back into him. "I'm trying to talk to you," I protested.

He stared into my eyes and I almost melted, but then I remembered who I was dealing with. "And I'm tryna get some head from yo' sexy ass."

I rolled my eyes in annoyance and fanned him away from me. "Boy bye."

Once I sat down on the sofa I thought he'd got the hint that I didn't want to be bothered. Of course that nigga didn't. Next thing I knew, he unzipped his jeans, whipped his dick out and held it less than a centimeter from my face. I took a whiff and immediately smelled the offensive stench of another bitch's fishy ass pussy. He'd just fucked some hoe and had the nerve to put his nasty ass dick close to my nose. My face was scrunched up into a frown less than a second later and he noticed.

"What the fuck…?" He asked.

"Your dick smells like some bitch's nasty ass pussy and you think I'm gon' suck it! You could've at least washed that shit, but nah, you ain't got one ounce of respect for me! Get yo' dirty dick outta my face nigga before I cut it off…for real. As a matter of fact get the fuck out! I'm done with yo' sorry ass!" I rolled my eyes at that disrespectful ass nigga and walked away.

He was on my heels, but he didn't put any fear in my heart. When I turned around there was a sneaky ass smirk on his face that suddenly turned into an angry scowl.

"Done wit' me?" He doubled over with laughter and even slapped his knee for emphasis. "You one funny bitch."

I just stared at him with my mouth wide open.

"You must've forgot who the fuck my daddy is. You won't be breathing long, let alone laughing after this...bitch!" I snapped.

He looked at me and there that sly ass smile that he was infamous for was again. "Oh, believe me shawty, I ain't forgot a damn thang," he said.

I went and sat down again. When he tried to put his used up dick on my lips, I pursed them together and turned away defiantly. My hands were pushing his body away as I moved my face from side to side. I was avoiding the assault of the dick that I used to crave. It took no time for me to see through Trell and I wished I'd seen clearly sooner. Thinking he'd matured and changed over the years had caused me to make a fucked up decision.

"I'm gon' tell my..."

My heart dropped down to my size 7 Red Bottoms when he grabbed me, pulled me up from the sofa and put his hand over my mouth. Hot tears spilled down my cheeks against my will.

"Shut up bitch! You ain't gon' tell a goddamn thang! Now shut the fuck up before I shoot you in yo' head up in this bitch!" His fingers were around my neck and I couldn't breathe. "Mendosa ain't here to help you now. Is he?

"Stop...Trell...stop..." I choked and tried to gasp for air.

I felt the cold steel of the gun that he was holding against my neck. That was odd. Anytime I thought of someone pointing a gun I thought of the head or chest, but he was ready to hit my jugular and just get it over with.

He finally let me go, put the gun in the waist of his jeans and then stared deep into my eyes. "It ain't that easy to leave me Sen." All of a sudden he looked dead ass serious again. His eyes were dark and empty, like a serpent. Damn, he was crazier than I thought.

Instead of warning Trell again and further pissing him off, I made a mental note to finally tell my father the truth about him. That nut case was psycho and I wasn't going to underestimate him. He knew that my father didn't play those games when it came to me. There had to be something really wrong with him mentally for him to point a gun at me and threaten my life. I knew that he sniffed coke and did Molly from time to time. Well, that was among a cocktail of other shit that he used to get high. Was he really ready for the war that my father was going to wage against him for fucking with me?

Once I officially knew that Trell was gone in the head it was already too late. I was a codependent person who felt the need to be needed by somebody. At first that was how Trell made me feel. It was like we were old friends reuniting. I couldn't trust too many people, so knowing that we'd grown up together gave me a feeling of familiarity. That was over quick, fast and in a hurry.

"You can't force me to be with you," I managed to get out when I finally got my breathing back to normal. "Especially not after this. How you gon' come in here wit' yo' dick smellin' like some diseased ass hoe and then get mad at me 'cause I don't wanna suck it! Sorry ass. Then you gon' point a gun at me!" I couldn't believe that nigga. He was brave as fuck.

He let out a cocky laugh. "Bitch, I'll fuck whoever I want and you gon' still suck my dick! I'll do whatever I want to yo' ass! You gon' stay wit' me too, 'cause you ain't got no choice."

It was my turn to laugh, but it was full of sarcasm. "Oh, I got a choice muthafucka."

He paced the floor and then glanced over at me before stopping to stare. "You're so fuckin' beautiful Sen. I mean, I don't mean to hurt you, but that's just how I am baby. I'm a fucked up nigga. When I love a bitch, I do what I gotta do to keep her. I been wantin' you since we were kids and I ain't lettin' you go that easy ma. Hell nah"

"Oh, so you want me to believe that you love me while referring to me as a bitch. Seriously Trell, you need to leave…" I pulled my cell phone from my back pocket to call my dad and thought about the 380 in a drawer in my bedroom.

As much as I wanted to go get it, I wondered if I'd catch a bullet in my back first.

"Go ahead and call Mendosa. You think I'm scared of his old, has been ass? If so, I'm sorry baby girl, but yo' ass got me all fucked up. As a matter of fact, I'm 'bout to prove that you ain't goin' nowhere and I'm yo' daddy now." He snatched the phone from my hand, ended the call, and winked at me with that gun still in his hand. I felt like throwing up. What the hell had I gotten myself into?

* * *

It took everything in me to go along with Trell until he trusted that I wasn't going to defy him. The longest night of my life was finally over after six tortuous hours.

He had literally raped me and I was all cried out by the time the sun had come up. My mind was on vengeance at that point and no matter what he'd shown me or done, I had to stop him. Fear made me want to fight back. Mendosa was my father and that didn't seem like a perk in my situation. I wanted to tell him, but that nigga Trell was black mailing me.

"Remember that there're consequences if you leave me bitch. You already know what'll happen and shit. If your father finds out about us, you better convince him that we're in love. If not, you know what's gonna happen to yo' ass. There's something else I want you to do, but we'll talk about that later. I'm watchin' you ma. Do you think it was really a fuckin' coincidence that I ran into you at that club?" He chuckled. "Hell nah ma. I'm a mufuckin' calculated nigga. I got plans for you."

Butterflies danced in the pit of my stomach and I had to swallow to keep the bile down. When the door finally closed I locked it and the tears started again as I slid down to the floor. Why the hell was my life being turned upside down? What Trell had just revealed had made shit even harder for me than they already were. Everything was piling up on top of my head and I was suffocating in my mistakes.

* * *

A few hours had passed since Trell had gone and I was shook for real for the first time in my adult life. Now that I thought about it, it was probably the second time. I mean, I'd been leery before of what my choices would bring to me, but things were different now. He had actually shown me something that had left my mouth wide opened with sheer shock. That nigga knew that he had something that could stop my world...and not only mine, but my father's too.

When my phone rang I hoped that it wasn't Trell. Tears were falling from my eyes nonstop since he left and I was actually afraid to even leave my condo. Usually I could use my father as my shield of protection, but not that time. I just knew that Trell was watching my every move. Calling my father crossed my mind, but then I thought about what my so called boyfriend was holding over my head. I didn't recognize the number, but I decided to answer anyway.

Clearing my throat, I let out a soft, "Hello." I was trying to sound normal and hoped that I did.

"Sen? It's Keenyn."

"Keys," I let out a breath in relief. Thank God it was him. "How're you doing?"

"I'm good. I meant to call you earlier, but it's been a lot going on. What you doin' tonight?" He asked and I could tell that he wanted to see me.

"It's cool. I understand. Nothing much. Netflix and ice cream." Honestly the television was off and I had no appetite.

There I was, a beautiful woman with money in my early twenties and my life was slowly, but surely going to shit. I was supposed to be out on the town enjoying myself, but I was hiding out from a nigga who wanted to destroy me for whatever reason. Trell had his own agenda the whole time and it had never been about me. I had no idea what else he had under his sleeve, but I was sure that it was going to be at my expense.

"Word, word. Why don't I come check you out? I mean, I have to be honest, I can't stop thinkin' 'bout you. I mean, I'm not tryna push up on you. I just wanna chill wit' you for a lil' while. No pressure. I promise."

I smiled, but I knew that it wasn't a good idea. Calling my mother had crossed my mind so that she could smuggle me out of Atlanta and send me to another safe haven. Maybe it was best for me to relocate again. I couldn't go back to Miami though. It was too much going on and I was running away from something that I could only pray wouldn't catch up to me.

"Well, I uh, I'm gonna be honest wit' you Keys. I got a...boyfriend who lives here...and..."

He cut me off. "Oh, damn, nuff said shawty...I..."

"But that doesn't mean that I can't kick it with you. I'll come to you," I said quickly. All a sudden I felt brave.

Maybe I could call Trell and throw him off. If I told him that I was going to sleep and went along with his plan, maybe he'd leave me alone for the night. The thought of being with Keys made me feel safe.

"Cool, uhh, I'll text you my address."

"Okay."

"See you in a minute."

"A'ight."

We hung up and I dialed Trell's number.

"Sexy, you thought about what we talked about huh?" He asked like nothing had even happened earlier.

I wanted to blow his brain out of his head myself, but what he'd showed me made me change my mind. Maybe I could tell Keys all about everything and he could help me. That nigga Trell had some shit on my pops that could get him locked up for life, or worse. Trell had it all covered. He said that if I told my father anything his crew had the word to take shit to the next level. That meant ending my life and my father's. Prison seemed to be the least of my worries and his.

"Yeah. I just wanted to call and tell you goodnight. I'm goin' to bed." I yawned to drive my point.

"Okay cool. I'll be there to check up on you in the mornin'. I'm handlin' some shit, so…"

"It's okay. My pops is comin' over in the mornin' and I don't think you should be here. I'll call you when he leaves."

"Yeah, what the fuck ever yo'. I'll pop up over there if I want to. Like I said bitch, I'm yo' daddy now. You better be in the bed too. You don't know if I'm goin' ride by to see if yo' car there. Try me if you want to Sen." His sinister voice made chills travel all over my body.

"Okay," I said making a mental note to call a taxi just in case he went through with his threat.

* * *

Keenyn

Damn, I shook my head when I thought about Jasenia having a nigga. That shit was a huge disappointment and I wasn't trying to be her side nigga too. I'd been through that bullshit with Elena, but at least Jasenia had been honest with me. It had been twenty or so minutes since we talked. I had a glass of Hennessey and was twisting a blunt when my phone rang.

"I'll be there in a few minutes," her familiar voice greeted my ear and I smiled although her news of having a boo threw me for a loop.

"Okay. Did you eat? I got some Chinese food that I picked up on my way back from Dame's."

"Yeah, I did, but I need to smoke. I know you got something. I'm sure I'll get the munchies after that."

We laughed. "You right on time shawty."

After we hung up I made my rounds to see if the crib was straight. I had to make sure that my bathroom was clean and my kitchen was up to par. Women like Sen didn't play that nasty shit. She was used to the finest and whether she had a nigga or not, I wanted to impress her sexy ass. Shit, I wanted her bad. Way more than I ever wanted Elena. For some reason I was willing to fight for her.

About fifteen minutes passed before the doorbell rang. I looked through the peephole and saw her standing there looking like a fallen angel. Damn, I was willing to go through whatever I had to just to get next to her. Without hesitation I opened the door and let her step in before pulling her enticing body into mine for an embrace.

She seemed surprised by my gesture, but not in a bad way. Soon I felt her body relax against mine and I held her even tighter. For some reason I got the vibe that she needed that hug. After I kissed her on the forehead, I finally let her go.

"What's a beautiful woman like you doing at home watching Netflix and eating ice cream when you got a man? The only reason I ain't takin' you out on the town is cuz I don't wanna have to kill a nigga."

She shook her head with a smile on her face, but there was something in her eyes that didn't match it. I wanted to know what was up with her, but I didn't pry. It wasn't like we'd been in touch over the years. We'd just reconnected, so I didn't want to push her to reveal too much of herself. I'd give her time. Besides, she had a man. Damn.

I led her to the sofa and we both took a seat. After lighting a blunt we engaged in conversation. Sen was so damn smart and everything we talked about was deep. Nothing at all about the conversation was superficial, but she didn't tell me anything about herself.

"Of course I know all about Black Wall Street and the Tulsa Race Riots. It happened in 1921 in Oklahoma," Sen challenged me when I asked. "Don't think just because I had an education abroad that I'm not up on my Black History sir. It was a sophisticated system of keeping our money in our own community. Businesses were booming and everybody was wealthy. There were doctors, lawyers, teachers, schools, stores and hospitals. Even indoor plumbing until those jealous ass, cracker ass KKK ruined it with their bombs and shit."

There was an angry look on her face.

"Well, excuse me for insulting your intelligence ma." I couldn't help but smile because when I brought that up to Elena she didn't know what the hell I was talking about.

"I'm high as hell," she sighed. "You said you got some Chinese food right?"

I couldn't help but stare at her. "You're so damn pretty and smart as fuck too. Why your man ain't checkin' for you?"

Her eyes suddenly misted over with tears, but she seemed to keep them at bay.

"What's wrong Sen?"

She shook her head quickly. "Nothing...I uh..."

"What's up wit' yo' nigga? When I brought him up your eyes changed." I shook my head as I grabbed her hand. "I know I haven't seen you in years, but I'll always have your back Sen. You can tell me anything baby girl." I had a feeling that whoever she was with was a conflict of interest when it came to Mendosa.

In her father's eyes, she was off limits to any man, but something told me that the situation that she was in was a lot more...complicated. I had a feeling that if her pops found out who her man was, it was going to be a major fucking problem.

"Let me enjoy my high Keys, okay." She squeezed my hand and the light was suddenly back on behind her eyes.

I reluctantly let it go and got up to fix us both a plate of food. I'd let it go for the moment, but I had to know what was going on with her. When I returned to the room she was puffing on one of those electronic cigarettes. It was all high tech looking and shit with a glass tank and a bright orange battery.

"You smoke that shit?" I asked wondering about the contraption.

"It's called vaping," she informed me with a cute giggle. "I used to smoke cigarettes, but I don't like the way they smell."

"You trust that shit?"

She shrugged her shoulders. "I figure I gotta die from something right."

"But you wanna find cures for diseases. Why would you say that?"

She sat her plate on her lap and dug in before answering me. "Lighten up Keys. I'm not trying to kill myself."

"You better not be…" My voice trailed off as my eyes focused on a faint scar on her wrist.

I wanted to ask if she'd tried already, but I didn't. My heart ached for her because a voice deep inside of my being told me that the beautiful, pampered princess had not had an easy life. Instead of focusing on the fucked up shit, I decided to be that friend that she needed.

We talked more and enjoyed our meal of beef and broccoli with shrimp spring rolls. After a few shots of Avion Silver she fell asleep on the sofa. I watched her sleep peacefully for a few minutes, enjoying the gift of her beauty. Then I gently picked her up and placed her in my bed. After covering her up with the blanket I went into the living room and sprawled out on the sofa. All I could think about was Jasenia as I drifted off to sleep.

Chapter 6

Jasenia
3 years ago
Miami, FLA

"You're at that school around all those pretty young bitches all day," my mother said as she sipped Chardonnay from a crystal goblet.

We were having dinner on a Sunday evening, which was our thing since I'd officially moved back home a year ago. During my entire childhood I was away. Sometimes I wondered if my mother even wanted to be around me. After expressing my feelings to her she decided that we should work on bonding. I looked like my father and so...I felt she resented me. It was like looking at me hurt her, so after they divorced, she sent me away.

"What does that have to do with anything?" I speared a perfect piece of salmon and savored the flavor.

My mom had always been a good cook, but being a good mother was a whole different story. She'd always been around physically when I was in the States, but emotionally she was disconnected. It was like she couldn't bond with me. My father and I were closer. He often told me that he and my mom broke up because she was jealous of our relationship. She felt that he gave me way too much of his attention and she got none. He said that when she finally decided to leave he asked to have custody of me. She never really wanted children anyway. She'd even admitted that fact to me time and time again. I was born because she wanted to keep him. He wanted children, so...The thought made me shake my head.

My mother only kept me with her after they split to get at my father. She sent me away only to keep me away from him. Well, I guess she wanted me away from her too. I resented her for that shit. Although I had the best education that money could buy, and I'd been exposed to places and things that most black girls my age didn't get to see, it didn't matter. That was time that I could've had with my father; the parent who truly loved me.

"Well, you know that it's time for you to pull your weight. It hasn't been cheap raising you." Her mouth was in a tight line as her golden brown eyes twinkled with mischief.

My mother was delicately beautiful at 5'5, 135 toned and fit pounds. She kind of reminded me of the actress Dorothy Dandridge with her classic beauty and poise. Her honey toned complexion was flawless and her slender nose was the result of a nose job my father had paid for. She'd also had breast implants and a Brazilian Butt Lift at his expense. However, my mother was a walking contradiction. Her beauty was her weapon and she was a deadly woman. Loving money was her vice. She was conceited as hell and she was a master manipulator. Using that to her advantage, she decided to become a female pimp. She'd been running an escort service since I was thirteen.

"What?" I dropped my fork. "I have a full scholarship mom...Daddy fronts the bill for everything. What have you paid for? It's not like you even raised me. Every dime you've ever made you've only spent on yourself!"

"You ungrateful bitch!" She yelled as she slammed her fist on the table in anger.

I looked up at her in disbelief. "What the fuck? Are you serious right now! I'm an ungrateful bitch? You should've left me in Atlanta with my father! You don't give a shit about me!"

She seemed to calm down as she took a deep breath. Her tone wasn't as harsh when she spoke again. "I'm sorry honey. I am...really."

My breathing was labored because I wanted to haul off and slap the shit out of her. Because of her ass I was emotionally scarred. She never put her hands on me, but she had been mentally abusive since I was a little girl. Not only that, but she had a way of pushing me away. I felt so neglected and abandoned. When I was with my father, I genuinely felt loved.

"Whatever. Thanks for dinner, but I have to go. I have finals tomorrow and..."

"Jasenia, I...well..." Suddenly the aggressive woman I'd known all my life seemed at a loss for words.

"What is it mom?" I was annoyed and all I wanted to do was leave.

"Well, I know that you love money too. You've always been so loyal to your father, but what about me?" That made me flinch. She couldn't be for real. I didn't say a word as she continued to talk.

"I mean, why don't you recruit some girls for me. I'll make it worth your while. You're driving that nice ass Benz and you stay flyy like your mama. Flash those designer bags. Why don't you carry one of those Ferragamo bags that your daddy bought you? Entice those bitches. You can make a gwap baby girl. Listen to your mama."

I gave her a wicked look before I got up from the table. "I'll call you later...mama."

She didn't say anything as I left and slammed the door behind me. So, she wanted me to help her exploit young women who were struggling to get an education. That was the whole point of our little dinners. All I could do was shake my head. What would my father think if he knew that my mother was trying to pull me into her illegal way of life?

She made a lot of money and all, but I'd never wanted any part of what she did. The money was tempting though, so I thought about it as I unlocked the door of my Benz. My phone buzzed inside of my purse, but I didn't answer. I knew that it was my mother...Missy...the Madame.

* * *

When my eyes fluttered open and I looked around the room anxiety quickly set in. Where the fuck was I?

My focus wasn't really working and my head was hurting like hell.

"Shit," I whispered when I sat up and realized that the unfamiliar looking room was spinning.

Damn, I hoped I hadn't fucked a strange ass nigga again. All of a sudden I felt nauseous as hell when the events of the night before came rolling into my mental. The images of what Trell had shown me was making me trip. Suddenly I was in a panic and I was hyperventilating.

Calm down, I told myself as I squeezed my eyes closed. I had to think. Okay, I was at Keenyn's, so I must've been in his bedroom. It was all coming to me. We'd had a nice time talking and vibing, but deep down inside I wanted to spill my guts to him. I wanted to tell him everything. I wanted to start from the beginning, but could I trust him? Shit, could I trust anybody other than my father?

I took deep breaths like my therapist had showed me. Years had passed since I'd seen her. I'd been dealing with my anxiety attacks really well lately, but shit was starting to hit the fan. There was no way I could go on the way that I was. I was a strong bitch, but even strong bitches could fold under pressure. Time and time again I'd been a victim of that shit.

My nausea subsided and I stood up on wobbly legs realizing that I had all of my clothes on. Good, that meant I hadn't fucked Keys. Thank God. I mean, he was attractive as hell and intelligent, but I couldn't go there. It would make things too damn complicated. My fucked up ass life didn't need any more complications. I was living, walking proof that money didn't buy happiness. With access to plenty of it, I was a mess.

There was soft knock at the door. "You okay in there?"

"Yes," I called out loud enough for him to hear.

"Uh, it's a pack of toothbrushes in the bathroom and I cooked some breakfast."

I almost laughed. A pack of toothbrushes? Who did that? It was thoughtful though to think of your guests. He must've had bitches over often.

"Thank you!"

I walked into the master bathroom and found the toothbrushes in a drawer. After brushing my teeth and washing my face, I tried to brush my weave. It was time for me to get my hair done. Wearing a sew-in was easy, but my real hair needed to breath. I made a note to self to handle that as soon as I got my head straight.

After getting myself together the best I could, I ventured out of the bedroom. Keenyn was sitting at the table and there was a plate beside him waiting for me. I smiled, but it was short lived.

"You made it," he said with a grin as I joined him.

"Yeah, thank you."

"For what?" He asked. "You ain't gotta thank me."

"For being a friend. Mmm, this looks good. You're gonna get me fat."

I looked down at the scrambled eggs, toast, grits and turkey sausage links and said grace before digging in.

"I like thickness baby girl," he laughed.

I laughed too and the food was good. We talked a little bit between bites and then an overwhelming feeling to get something off my chest took over me.

"Can I trust you Keys?"

He glanced over at me in surprise. "Hell yeah. Why'd you ask me that?"

"It's been a lot going on and so I have trust issues. Honestly, I can only trust my father. I need to know that I can trust you too." The tears burned my eyes and I willed them away. Yet, still, they fell.

"What's wrong?" Keys asked with his hand on my shoulder. "I knew it was something Sen. Please, you can talk to me."

I peered up at him and decided to go ahead. Shit, what did I have to lose? It couldn't get any worse.

"You know Trell right?" I asked.

"Rocky?" His brows furrowed together and then he frowned. "Yeah, why?"

I sighed and then cleared my throat. "He's my boyfriend."

"Fuck," he whispered before getting up to clear the table.

"Come sit down Keys. Let me finish."

He sat down beside me and from the look on his face, I could tell that the news was unsettling. I had to ask.

"Are ya'll still cool?"

"Hell nah. We fell out a long ass time ago."

"I hope that doesn't affect our friendship."

"How long you been wit' that reckless ass fool. I know how Mendosa feels about him. He wants to take over his territory ma. What the fuck?" He shook his head in disbelief. "You gotta know that..."

"Now I do, but at first I didn't know how serious it was. My father doesn't tell me everything. He's the closest person to me, but still, my resentful, rebellious nature made me not care that he doesn't like Trell. I had no clue it was that deep though. Not until last night."

"What happened Sen? You can trust me. I'm dead ass serious. Just talk to me."

I believed him, so I continued. "I noticed that he was changing a couple months ago. Bitches were calling his phone all times of night and he was starting to get all disrespectful. I wanted to end things with him last night, but things didn't go as planned." The tears started again, but I wiped them away and pushed myself to get it out. "He actually put a gun to my neck. I was so scared for my life. He even forced himself on me."

"That nigga raped you? Shit ma, why didn't you tell Mendosa about this? He'll..." His face was balled up. "I'll kill that bitch ass nigga."

"I thought about telling my father Keys. Believe me, I have. The only thing is he has something on my dad. He showed me a video that he uploaded on to his phone, but it had no sound. It's surveillance of his father's house. He said that he had several cameras outside and inside of the house. Five years ago his father disappeared and his body was never found. My father killed him. I could see him clear as day. He choked him out and that nigga Trell found the video a year ago. After his pops was reported missing his uncle broke down the surveillance cameras and took all of the footage out of fear of the cops finding something incriminating during their investigation. Trell found the videos, watched the footage and saw my father choke his father to death and then put him in the trunk of his car. He said if I ever leave him, or say anything to my father about what he'd done to me he'll report the murder to the police and then kill me and my entire family. He said he'll kill anybody close to me. Now I'm waiting for him to tell me what else he wants me to do for him. I have no clue what that is. I can't let my father get locked up for murder and I can't risk getting anybody that I love killed. I have to kill Trell, but I have to do it the right way. His boys are psycho. I don't want them to come after me or my father. I know my pops can hold his own, but damn. He's getting older Keys." I couldn't hold my tears back anymore. "Trell said that his crew has the word to carry on his plan even if he does get killed. I don't know what the fuck to do. You have to help me"

Keys wrapped his arms around me and held me close to him as I sobbed. "I remember when his pops first went missin' ma. They still ain't found his body."

"He's been holding on to what he knows to black mail me into being with him. I got a feeling he's gonna use me to go through with his take over. He thinks I can help him take over the East Side."

"I ain't as shocked as I should be because one thing I knew about Trell is the fact that he can be a scheming ass nigga. He must've targeted you on purpose. How could you be so naïve? Why the hell would you deal wit' a nigga that Mendosa's always warned you about? You had to know it was something fishy as hell about that nigga poppin' up at the same club you was at. Keys shook his head. "We gotta go tell your pops."

I gave him a desperate look. "We can't tell him Keys and I trust you not to behind my back."

"Damn Sen. That nigga ain't invincible and his crew ain't either. Shit a few bullets can end all this shit." I could tell that he was mad as hell that I was letting that nigga Trell have the upper hand.

There was a faraway look in his eyes.

"To answer your question, I didn't really know anything about Trell. My father never told me that he was his rival. Honestly, I hadn't heard him say anything about him lately. When I started dealing with Trell it was because I felt like I knew him since we did kind of grow up together. It wasn't me being naïve. I was being rebellious." I sighed and continued. "I'd never, ever gone against my father about anything. When he started fucking with that bitch Sybil we went to school with..."

"What? Mendosa was fuckin' Sybil Lyons? I had no clue about that shit," Keys said shaking his head.

"Yeah, and I found out about it a few months before I saw Trell. I figured if my pops could fuck a bitch my age, I'd fuck a nigga he didn't like. Well, he left Sybil alone, but now I'm stuck with Trell. If I had known that he had ambitions to fuck my father over, none of this bullshit would be happening. I just wish my father would've been honest with me. I mean, he didn't really like Trell when we were kids, but I didn't think it was that damn deep. I didn't know that the shit was life or death Keys." Burying my face in my hands, I cried. "Please, don't tell my father."

"What do you want me to do then Sen? I'll do whatever I can to protect you, but damn...You know that your pops is better equipped to handle this shit than you and me. I can get my boy Dame in on it, since he don't like Trell, but I don't know if not tellin' Mendosa is a good decision."

I pulled away from him, but he pulled me back. My body shook and convulsed with each sob and he rubbed my back softly in an attempt to calm me down. In a few minutes it seemed like it was working. My warm breath tickled his ear as I whispered, "I wish you'd showed up at the club that night instead of him. Things

would be so different now." I sighed. He smelled so
damn good.

"Me too shawty, me too. Why don't you want
Mendosa to know the truth?"

"Because, he's gonna be disappointed in me.
Then it's the possibility of him getting locked up, or
killed. I can't chance it. I have to handle Trell myself. I
got me and my father into this shit and I'm gonna get us
out of it."

Then I thought about it. I had to leave. I'd almost
forgotten that he was supposed to be coming to my place
to check things out. Part of me wanted to tell him the
truth then, but I couldn't take that chance. I had to finesse
the situation to my advantage. In the meantime I would
just have to pretend that I was going along with Trell's
twisted plot.

"Okay," Keys said softly and then pulled away
from me. "I'm gonna come up wit' a way to help you and
you got my word that I won't say shit."

I nodded as I attempted to get myself together.
My father had called and left a voicemail asking for my
address.

"Thanks Keys, but I have to go. My dad's coming
over to check out my neighborhood." I rolled my eyes
and stood up.

"Okay, I'll walk you to your car." Keys stood up
too. "I wanna make sure everything's good just in case."

I shook my head and thought about it. "Damn, I
didn't drive."

"How'd you get here?" Keys' eyes were curious.

"A taxi." I dialed a number on my cell.

"Nah yo'. I'm takin' you home."

"No," I spoke up quickly. "I don't know if Trell's watching me or not. That's why I didn't drive. Don't worry. I'll call a taxi."

Keys sighed and sat back down. "Okay."

After I called the taxi I sat down too and the room was dead silent. The anxiety of my father being in the same place that Trell had assaulted me and not being able to tell him had set in. How in the hell could I keep something like that from him? Damn, it was hard, but I was determined not to cry again. I had to do whatever was necessary to make sure that Trell didn't succeed in his plan and my father never found out about us. I had to let go of that emotional shit and show that nigga Trell that I was Mendosa's daughter and I didn't take no shit either.

* * *

After sending Keys a text letting him know that I'd made it safely and I'd call him later, my phone rang.

"Mother, how are you?" I asked with a cynical edge to my voice.

The two of us had always coexisted, but never really were close. My mother's past was layered in dysfunction and she'd pushed the same bullshit into my life. When I was a little girl she never hugged me or told me that she loved me. I got all of my affection and validation from my father. In my mind I didn't think she cared about me one bit.

"I'm well and yourself?" She sounded bitter and resentful although she tried to disguise it.

"Could be better actually."

She cleared her throat at my sentiment.

"Hmm, well, I was just calling to check up on you and shit. Uh, has anything…happened?" She asked sounding concerned, but I didn't know if she really was.

"No, as a matter of fact, the crazy shit I'm going through right now has nothing to do with what happened in Miami." It just slipped out, but I didn't plan on divulging the details of my problems with Trell to my mother. She held on to whatever information she wanted to hold on to, but she would surely tell my father about that.

"What? What the hell's going on Jasenia?"

"Nothing. I'm fine. Nobody's coming after me…if that's what you want to know. What about you?" Saying too much over the phone was not a good idea.

She was staying in a nice, Spanish style vista in Puerto Rico. We'd both fled from Miami in an attempt to stay alive. The business of prostitution was just as ruthless as drug dealing and I'd learned that shit the hard way. Neither of us wanted my father to know about that either. My mother knew that my father would never approve of what she'd asked of me.

"Things seem to be fine on my end." She sighed. "How's your father?"

"He's ok. He'll be here in a little while. He has to make sure I'm in a safe area. Security and a gate are not enough." I let out a sarcastic laugh.

I wished I never gave Trell the gate's security code. It was ironic that my father was so over protective, but he couldn't protect me from the shambles my life was in now.

"Well, you know how your father is over you. You've always been his world." She sounded resentful as hell when she said it. "Just make sure you keep your mouth shut about what happened. It's no telling what he'd do to me."

For some reason I didn't feel sorry for her. Not one bit. Yet and still, it was my fault that I'd fallen for her bullshit manipulation. I'd let her convince me that doing her bidding would be worth my while. Well, it wasn't. Now I was running away from some shit that I could've avoided. Maybe being away from her all those years had been the best thing for me. Being exposed to that bitch had ruined my life. I only dealt with her because, after all, she was my mother.

"He won't find out, if you deal with it like you said you were going to." I was frustrated because I was on the run for my life because of her greed.

"I'm dealing with it. It's just not as easy as I thought it would be."

I was already tired of the conversation. "I'll call you back mother. Just do what you said so I can go on with my life."

"Well, I'm sorry if life isn't all bubble gum dreams and princesses like your father led you to believe. I always tried to show you tough love so you'd know how to deal with shit like this!" She huffed.

"I can't believe you woman!" I calmed myself down. "If we weren't on the phone I'd tell you how the fuck I really feel. I'm hanging up now. Just handle it. Okay."

She hung up without saying anything else. I tried to contain myself and took a few deep breaths. Damn, I really needed a drink, but it was early as hell. Shit, I didn't care. I poured myself a shot of Patron and then another before rinsing with mouthwash. My dad would go off if he smelled alcohol on my breath so early.

The doorbell rang and I rushed to answer hoping that Trell wasn't lurking around somewhere.

"Hi daddy," I said before kissing his cheek.

I'd given him the code to open the gate before he got there and he was pleased to know that I lived in a gated community. Still, knowing that Trell had the code too made me not feel as safe as he thought I was. The fact that Trell wasn't my only threat made me feel even worse.

"Hey sweetie." He stepped inside and closed the door behind him.

Without saying anything else to me, he gave himself a quick tour without my help. When he returned to where I was he had a look of approval on his face.

"Good to see that ain't no nigga's clothes in your closet." He chuckled.

I shook my head. "I'm a grown woman daddy. You and mom were living together at my age. Why can't I have someone?"

"You can. Just not right now. Look at what happened to me and your mom. We rushed into it. Take your time to experience life first."

His advice sounded good, but to be honest, I'd already experienced enough of life. After the things I'd been through in my short 21 years, I felt that I was ready for just about any damn thing. My mind drifted away to the reality of it all. My life was in danger and there wasn't just one threat against it. I had made a few enemies and my father, the infamous killer Mendosa, couldn't even help me.

Chapter 7

Keenyn

I had that Kevin Gates on full blast in the whip. A nigga couldn't help but rap along with him. At that point I was so hyped that I didn't even care that I had seven pounds in a secret 007 compartment under the dashboard. Shit, seven was my lucky number.

"24 hours, nigga, 7 days a week
me, I don't get tired, I let you other niggas sleep.
Turn up for that check and yeah I get it out the streets.
Hustle like I'm starving going hard, I gotta eat.
I get it out the mud, yeah, yeah.
I get it out the mud, yeah, yeah, yeah.
Watch how I break my wrist.
Make that water whip.
Stretch it out, then flip.
I'm all about my chips!"

That was my shit and it got me so hype that I almost didn't see twelve on the side of the road. I quickly turned the volume down and slowly eased my foot off the gas. I didn't hit the brake though. I hated when people did that dumb, scary ass shit. It wasn't like I was speeding, but if I didn't see that nigga I would've been.

Good, he didn't follow me. I wanted to wipe the sweat from my forehead that had suddenly accumulated. My nerves were fucked up and I shook my head thinking about how niggas like Dame fucked with that real dope.

If I was paranoid as hell with a few pounds of green, I could only imagine what those niggas went through.

Less than ten minutes later my GPS told me that I was at my destination. I pulled up and parallel parked so I could just get the fuck up out when I was ready. After pulling my cell out of my pocket, I pulled up my contacts and hit John Gotti.

"Yeah," a throaty voice answered.

"Outside my nigga."

"A'ight, c'mon to the door. My neighbors nosey as hell."

I grabbed the shit from its hiding spot and put the strap from the bag on my shoulder. I'd been dealing with that nigga for years. He was an older cat who my pops used to serve. The thing was, he acted like he was my age. His name was really John, but he was an OG, so he adopted the Gotti part.

Although I'd done the same thing time and time again, I was always reluctant to get out of my car and go to a nigga's door. It wasn't because I feared any man, but clients were more of a threat than the police. The thing was, any kind of exchange of money could go south. Shit was often unpredictable and I could never know what a nigga was planning. Still, I'd been dealing with John long enough to trust him at least 50 percent. It was hard as hell to fully trust anybody when it came to drugs and money.

When I got inside he pounded me up and we made the exchange of weed and cash. I made sure that it was all there before heading back to my car. My phone rang and I noticed that it was Sen. I hadn't seen her in a couple days, but we'd talked off and on. It felt like my obligation to make sure that she was okay. She'd been doing a good job of keeping Trell at bay, but when I answered the phone she sounded frantic.

"I gotta see you," she said quickly. Her voice was laced with panic, but she was trying to hide it.

"Where you at?" I asked as I got behind the wheel and started the car up.

"On my way somewhere. I want you to meet me there so I'm gonna text you the address." Just like that she hung up.

As soon as the call ended my phone rang again. That time it was Dame.

"Yo."

"Sup mane? What's the word on that?"

"Ah shit man, not right now. I got something I gotta do." My mind was on Jasenia and what she needed to see me for. I had a feeling that things were really about to go left with her so called man.

"What? Nigga, you sound stupid as fuck! What is there to do other than make money?"

"I'm stupid nigga? Never. I won't even say what the fuck I think about you right now while you on this bullshit. When it comes to money I'm good a'ight. Don't worry 'bout my pockets mufucka. I told you I was gon' think about it. Well, I thought about it and I ain't dealin' wit' no new niggas. Tell them they gotta find somebody else to get that shit from."

Dame sighed like he was getting frustrated with me. "Talk to Mendosa for me man. See if he'll…"

"You already know he ain't fuckin' wit' that lil' shit nigga. C'mon now. Them niggas only want ten. He don't fuck wit' nothin' less than twenty unless it's me. Like I said, they gotta find somebody else."

"You a lame ass nigga yo. Straight the fuck up. For real. Now I'm gon' look like I don't make moves like I say I do. I told them niggas I was gon' hook them up wit' something and you on that bullshit. Niggas gon' think…"

"Shut the fuck up Dame. You always worryin' 'bout what other niggas gon' say. Be your own man nigga. Like I said, I been doin' shit like I been doin' shit and I ain't locked up, I'm above ground and I'm gettin' money my nigga. I got something to do. If them niggas trust you enough to give you the funds and I just fuck wit' you that's G, but I ain't fuckin' wit' them cats. I'on know them."

"A'ight man, damn," he said finally letting that shit go.

I figured they wouldn't be kosher with that, but if so, I was down.

"I'll hit you up later." I ended the call and shook my head.

Who the fuck did that nigga think he was running anyway? I needed him to help me come up with a way to get that nigga Trell, but lately he'd been on some other shit. It wasn't even like I could really talk about some serious shit with him. All he wanted to do was bark orders like I was part of his damn flunky crew. Like I needed him to make my ends. That nigga needed me.

After feeling pissed off for a few more minutes I checked my phone for the address that Jasenia had sent. It was located in McDonough, Ga, which was a forty minute drive. My guess was that she needed to get away from the city to elude Trell for a while.

I sent her a text letting her know that I was on my way. She didn't respond, but I headed to the address she'd sent anyway.

* * *

A narrow country road led to a huge gate similar to the one at Mendosa's. I pressed the button.

"It's Keys."

"Okay," Sen said softly and then the gate opened.

I drove in and the gate closed swiftly behind me. At that point I still couldn't see the house. A few yards ahead, I finally saw a two story, stone cottage style house. It was modern, but there were no neighbors for miles. There was also a silver Benz parked in the winding driveway. I parked behind it and anxiously got out of the car. Jogging toward the door, I noticed that it was opened, so I walked in.

"Come out back!" She called out.

That's when I noticed the glass slide door that led to a sparkling, infinity pool. I closed the door behind me and the security alarm beeped alerting me that the door had been closed. It also reminded me to lock it, which I did. Hmm, advanced system, I thought to myself. At that point I still couldn't see Sen.

After making my way out back where she was through the opened glass door, I was in awe of the scene. The backyard was like a tropical island with fake palm trees, a tiki pool bar, plenty of lights and a waterfall. However, the best part of the scenery was Sen's perfect body in a black, two piece bathing suit. My breath caught in my throat when I saw her.

"Well, damn." I shook my head and flashed a pitiful look. "Why you doin' this to a nigga?"

She smiled, but her eyes said something totally different. "What?"

"You know what. Don't act like you don't know what you look like."

A laugh rose from her throat, but she was serious again in an instant. "I'm not doing anything. I invited you out here, because I need to talk to you. Taking a swim was an afterthought. Water relaxes me. At this point I don't wanna chance us being seen together. Nobody really knows about this place. It's my mom's. She got it in the divorce settlement because my father got it built for her when they first got married. They lived here at first and then she got bored and wanted to move back to the city. Then he bought the house he lives in now. He said she was always fascinated with the houses in the fairytales she read as a child and so…" She waved her hand around. "This is the result."

I nodded in approval. "This place is straight yo'."

"Yeah, and it's well secured. Way better than my condo. At first I was just gonna move here. The only thing is, it's so… secluded. I'm thinking about staying out here until after Trell is…handled…but…I don't think I wanna be out here…alone." Her eyes got dark and misted over.

I was getting used to that and it made me feel like there was more bothering her than the situation with Trell. Instead of pushing her to open up to me, I was going to let her do it on her own. It was clear to me that she was damaged, but I wanted to fix her. Playing captain save a hoe wasn't my thing, but I knew that Sen wasn't a hoe. I'd known her for the first eleven years of her life. That was at least half of it. I knew who she *really* was deep down to her core. She was just a woman who was starving for love and I had enough for her to be a glutton.

"I still think it's best for you to stay here…for now."

She nodded. "I know. I've managed to avoid Trell's wrath for the past couple days. He thinks I'm in Miami handling some business about school. I whipped out my old Benz and left the Range at my father's. I know what he wants me to do now. He came over right before I supposedly left for Miami. Of course he had to let me know that he'll kill everybody I love if I'm up to something. The plan is for me to give him access to my father's reserve."

Mendosa's reserve would be the lick of a lifetime. He had to have at least 500 kilos of coke that he had got directly from an underground pipeline that led from Miami to Columbia. It was actually kept at an undisclosed location in barrels buried under the ground. Obviously Trell thought she knew where it was.

"Shit," I hissed.

"The thing is, I don't even know where his reserve is. I convinced Trell that I can find out to buy me some time. That nigga's trying to be all nice and shit now because he needs me." She shook her head with a look of disgust on her face. "I can't wait until he takes his last fuckin' breath Keys."

"Me either." I sighed picturing my nine in his mouth before blowing his brains out. "We just gotta make sure we do this shit right ma. I ain't scared to kill that nigga, but he got a lot of dumb ass mufuckas followin' his blind ass. The thing is, I ain't got no crew and I'on need one. A nigga like me be on my solo shit. I gotta make sure I'on make no stupid moves when it comes to murking that nigga. So, it's good that you bought some time for me to think. At first I was gonna put Dame in on it, but I think it's best we keep this shit under wraps."

She nodded. "I agree. You want a drink? Shit, I damn sure need one."

"Hell yeah." That shit was right on time.

The thought of Trell using her to fuck her own father over for his benefit had me heated. A drink would calm down my desire to go against all of my principles and go gun that nigga down right at that moment.

She walked inside as I pulled a baggie of Kush and a Swisher from my pocket. By the time she made it back out holding a tray with two glasses of ice, a bottle of Patron and some pineapple juice, I had the blunt already lit.

"Damn, that shit smells good." Regardless of what was going on she still managed to look relaxed.

"Yo' pops got that fiyah. I'on even smoke nobody else's shit. Never have."

"Hmm, that's that Jamaican connection."

"You ever been there?"

She nodded and sat down beside me at the patio table. "Plenty of times. I love it there."

"I never been," I said thoughtfully. "Always wanted to go though."

When she looked up at me her face lit up. "Well, I'm gonna have to take you one day."

She poured some Patron in both glasses, but when she twisted the top off of the pineapple juice and was about to pour some in mine, I stopped her. "Nah, straight for me shawty."

With a nod she pushed my drink toward me before adding just enough juice to add a little color to hers.

"Oh, I can drink too, believe me. I got a lot of demons to drown."

I thought about the scar on her wrist, but didn't bring it up. "Hmm," I clinked my glass against hers. "I'll toast to that shit."

"You ever been out of the US?" Sen asked after sipping her drink and taking a hit from the blunt I'd just passed her.

"Honestly, I've only been to Cancun once after I graduated from high school. Getting passports and shit ain't my thing. I'm a secretive nigga. They wanna know too much for you to go outta the country. I'm personally not tryna pay a nigga to do some fake shit for me and I get caught up on some fraud shit," I explained.

Sen gave me a look that told me that my logic was bogus. "Nigga, I can get you some official ass looking shit and we can go anywhere. I've been to 27 states and at least ten countries and I'm not done yet. I still have 23 states and who knows how many countries to go. I want to see the world. The world is so big Keys. Shit, I even wanna go out of space." Her face glowed and her eyes were huge with awe.

Damn, she looked incredible and I loved how her face became illuminated when she talked about something she was passionate about.

I was so amazed by her. "Wow ma, and you're only 22."

She sipped her drink again. "My mama loves to travel. That's the only time we really spend time together. My first flight was when I was six months old. Sky's been the limit ever since."

My glass was already empty by the time the blunt made it back to me. I took a toke and that shit tasted sweet as hell. Sen was quiet as she replenished our drinks. The sun was high in the sky and that pool actually looked inviting.

"Why y'en tell me about the pool and shit. I could've brought something to swim in."

She looked surprised. "You can swim?"

"Hell yeah," I chuckled. "I learned at the YMCA when we were kids. C'mon ma, you forgot? We learned how to swim together."

Her eyes were on me. "We damn sure did, but you can swim naked though." Suddenly she busted into hysterical laughter. "Now I remember Dame. Damian. He shitted in the pool that time. That shit was so fucking nasty. I remember we all got out of that bitch screaming."

My side was hurting because I was laughing so hard. "Damn shawty. I forgot about that shit."

"I remember something else," Sen suddenly said.

She passed the blunt to me and I studied her gorgeous face. Her eyes were pulling me in and I was under her spell. Damn, she wasn't even trying and a nigga was all in. Elena was a distant memory and all I could think about was the woman who was in front of me.

"What?"

There was a contemplative look lining her features. "I did come down one summer for two weeks when I was thirteen. You remember that?"

There was a sly glimmer in her eyes as she grinned sexily at me.

I did. "Oh...hell yeah...damn ma...I thought about that right after I saw you, but I ain't wanna bring it up. No pressure, remember?"

"Yeah," she said as I passed her the blunt. "But, I always wondered..."

"Me too..." I said remembering how we'd kissed and I'd fingered that tight, wet ass pussy for the first and last time.

She was gone two days later. I was still a virgin at that point and so was she. We'd wanted to be each other's first, but it just didn't happen. Ana had interrupted our little "play date" because Mendosa didn't want us to be unsupervised. The movie we had been watching didn't really seem that interesting anymore. I couldn't even remember what it was. I'd thought about Sen and what could've been for years, but eventually I let it go. Now, I wanted that again.

"Do you believe what they say about having a soul mate?" Her voice cut through my thoughts like a knife.

"Yeah," I said breathlessly. Maybe that explained why I couldn't really connect with anybody.

"Me too. I just didn't know that it was you until now Keys. I mean, I always thought about you. Never did I stop wondering what could've been with you. Then I think about my father and I know it would be damn near impossible for us to be together. I just gotta handle the mess I've made with my life before I can do anything else." Tears filled her eyes, but once again she didn't let them fall.

"You don't have to try to be so strong ma. It's okay to cry." So, she thought I was her soul mate? Shit, I was thinking the same thing.

She shook her head. "Mendosa's daughter has to be strong. Cry? For what. I don't cry. What does that solve? Crying doesn't fix shit."

"Maybe tryna be so damn strong is the problem. Why hold it in baby girl?"

"I'm not fragile Keys. I'm not a baby, nor am I a girl."

I grabbed her hand and kissed it. "I know, but you're still human. You got feelings and being Mendosa's daughter don't change that."

She pulled her hand away, wiped her eyes and forced a smile on her face. "Tell my mama that."

Her eyes dimmed again and the smile was gone. Without saying another word she stood up and walked toward the edge of the pool. She dived in and I was left to simmer about what she'd just said. Obviously she had a volatile relationship with her mother. Her father was clearly her ally and she was much closer to him. I wanted to know more, but I was going to wait patiently. So, I just sat there and watched her swim like a majestic mermaid, basking in her radiant beauty.

Chapter 8

Keenyn

My eyes were stuck on her when she finally rose from the water like a goddess. She stood in front of me as water dripped from her fine, sculptured body. I passed her the fluffy, white towel that was draped over the chair that she had been sitting in. She used it to dry off and I just stared at how her hair curled up and water droplets fell from the ringlets.

"You look mesmerized," she said with an amused look on her face.

"I am." My face was serious as hell because I wasn't playing no games with her sexy ass.

As she sat down, I continued, "Uh, about us being soul mates, I...well..."

"You're not a man of many words huh?" She proceeded to dry her hair.

"Well, not when it comes to...my feelings." I sighed and tried to find the right words to use. "I'm well...I never really cared about a chick. Well, maybe one...but... Uh, don't get me wrong, I get pussy." Suddenly I frowned, because that didn't really sound right since I was trying to get with her on that level.

"I mean, I'm into women, but I ain't never really had those real feelings. You know?"

She nodded and stared at me with curiosity as I tried to communicate the best way I knew how.

"Damn, ma, all I'm tryna say is, I'm feelin' something when I'm wit' you that I ain't never felt. It's, it's new and I like it. I ain't tryna fight it, 'cause it's a reason for everything and it's a reason that I'm here wit' you right now."

Her eyes were on mine and they were telling me that she was feeling the same way that I did.

"Now I understand why I couldn't really get into anybody else. I had to be available for you." Her voice was low and seductive and I was caught up.

Sen's aura was just too strong for words and I was lost in it. The struggle was real and my dick was hard as hell. Then I thought about that nigga Trell and how he was a certified hoe. I'd heard several rumors about bitches he'd fucked that were definitely A-Town thots. When I did hit, I wanted to feel that shit skin to skin, but I didn't want to have to worry about her giving me anything.

"I wanna go there wit' you Sen, but I gotta ask you something." Being a blunt nigga, I wasn't going to hold anything back.

She nodded and there was an anxious look on her face. "Okay."

"Uh, don't get offended by this shit. I'm just bein' real wit' mine and I hope you respect me for that. I care about you and I'll never put you in a fucked up situation. Especially when it comes to your life and shit. I hope you feel the same way about me. That nigga Trell, he, well, how can I put this?" I contemplated about a delicate way to tell her that the man she'd been in a relationship with would put his dick in anything.

"Just say it...please."

"Okay. Trell's fucked some of the nastiest bitches I know. Bitches most niggas wouldn't touch wit' another nigga's dick. All I'm sayin' is, before we go there, I gotta make sure you good. Have you ever let that nigga hit raw?" I wanted to know because when I did get up in it I didn't want no damn condom between us

She stared me straight in the eye. "Honestly, we've always used condoms and I'm not just saying that. Even when he called himself raping me he put on a condom. He said it was just in case I got brave and decided to report it. That nigga don't even eat pussy, so I'm good. I know that herpes and all that shit can be transferred with condoms, but I just went to the doctor a couple weeks ago and everything checked out. Oh and don't worry. I ain't never sucked his dick and I'm glad I didn't. I told him that would take a while." She looked a little embarrassed by the conversation, but I was glad it was all out.

"A'ight," I nodded believing her. "Now, if we...go there...it's over between you and that nigga. The sex is cut the fuck off."

"Shit, it's already over. I'm just gonna play it off as best I can until it's time to go along with whatever we're gonna do to get rid of his ass. And what do you mean *if* we go there. We're gonna go there. It's just a matter of time." She licked those thick, luscious lips and I couldn't help but stare.

"Okay sexy. I know you gotta do what you gotta do to make him think shit is all good, but you gon' stay away from his ass. I'd rather you stay at your pop's crib or here because I don't want him puttin' his hands on you again." My face was balled up into an angry frown and she blew me a kiss to calm me down.

"No worries. I'm gonna do what I gotta do, but he won't be fuckin' me again…"

"But he forced himself on you before and…"

"I told him that if he did that shit again I wasn't helping him. At first he got out of pocket talkin' about he'll give the cops the evidence before ending my life. He knows he'll rather get those kilos than get my pops locked up, or kill me right now. That's way more worth his while. I just gotta figure out a way to destroy his evidence. We gotta get our hands on his phone and the original video. Then we gotta find out if his boys are really on to that shit."

I thought about it. "You're right. Damn, we really can't just rush into that shit shawty. It's gonna take some real plannin' to pull that shit off."

"I know, but I'm glad I found you again. It's no way I could do this shit by myself. I…I…" Her voice trailed off.

Before the tears could start again I was on my feet making my way over to her. I pulled her up from her seat and pulled her body into mine. My embrace was crushing as I pressed her softness into my hard chest. Her arms were around my neck and mine were around her waist. Damn, I really wanted to palm that fat ass, but I kept my composure.

Resting her head on my chest she said in a soft, sweet voice, "You know exactly when to hug me."

I thought about that and it made me smile. "You used to say that when we were kids."

I felt her nod. "I know."

For a few minutes I just held her in silence and there were no tears in sight. That let me know that the moment of sadness had passed for now. I also knew that it would be back. It was clear that Sen was damaged, but she was beautifully damaged to me. Shit, we were all fucked up in a way, but I wanted to help her for some reason. Like an unfinished jigsaw puzzle, there were pieces of her that were out of place, but once she was whole, the result would be a stunning picture.

In the midst of my thoughts I felt her soft, warm hands on my face. I looked down at her and her eyes were full of the same longing that was in mine. My head dipped down to meet her waiting lips and then our tongues joined in a heated tango. It was like once we'd started we couldn't stop kissing.

"Damn," she whispered when I finally released her sweet mouth.

It felt like sparks were traveling all over my body and I was about to combust at any second. Shit, I had to adjust my hardness because I knew that my boy was stabbing her in the belly. He wanted to poke her somewhere else, but I wasn't going to rush her into anything.

As I licked my lips, she tightened her grip around me. "My body is literally on fire right now," she whispered.

"Shit, tell me about it," I agreed breathlessly. "You got me feelin' like I could do some real nasty ass shit to you right now."

She visibly shivered as my hands traveled up and down her back. It took everything in me to keep stopping at the slope of her ass. Mmm, I knew it was soft as hell. All I wanted was one little squeeze. I let my hand drop, since she'd let me kiss her. Without doing too much, I let the soft, silky material of her bathing suit linger under my touch. Damn, she felt so soft. I couldn't wait to touch her bare skin.

"Well, since we're askin' questions. Have you fucked any bitches raw?" She peered up at me.

"You the only woman I wanna hit raw ma. I slipped up in the past once or twice, but a nigga's good. I ain't one of them mufuckas who don't go to the doctor and shit. I make sure I'm straight. I strap up now for sho'. A nigga done seen some shit."

"Okay. Well, in that case what's stoppin' you from doin' the nasty shit you wanna do? Not me." Her voice was low, sexy and inviting.

"You sure?" I asked with my eyes glued to her face for a reaction.

Knowing that nigga Trell had raped her made me wonder if she'd be okay with me making love to her. I had no clue if she was emotionally, or physically fucked up behind it.

"I'm positive. This…is different. I want this." She knew exactly what my reservations were about.

The fact that she seemed to be able to read my mind made me kiss her fine ass again. That time I let both of my hands cup her ass cheeks.

"Mmm," I moaned in appreciation. A nigga was ready to take that bathing suit off of her.

There was also a gazebo in the back yard with a cushioned bench, so I grabbed her hand and led her to it. She sat down, but I wanted to see her body when I undressed her.

"Stand up," I coaxed. "I wanna see all of you."

She blushed and it made me wonder why she was being so bashful. It was not a secret that she was confident as hell, so I didn't know why she was acting all shy now.

"Believe me, it's just you. I'm nervous for some reason," she spoke up suddenly.

"Wow, can you read my mind shawty? Don't be nervous. Relax baby." I kissed her collar bone before removing her top.

When her perfectly round C cup breasts spilled out my mouth watered instantly. The big, brown nipples and dark areolas were begging to be touched and tasted. I

did both. Her hands softly caressed my face as I suckled
on each of her nipples like I was a new born baby.

"Damn, that feels so good." Her voice was raspy
and sensual.

It turned me on and sent a sudden wave of shivers
down my spine. I'd never been so physically into a
woman before in my life. Foreplay was my thing, but I
couldn't wait to get inside of her. It felt like I would
explode with anticipation I was so anxious.

My tongue danced all over the soft, warm flesh of
her flat stomach. I slurped her little innie belly button as
my fingers slipped inside of the waist band of her bathing
suit bottom. As I slid it down she helped me remove it by
stepping out of it one foot at a time. Once it was off my
eyes were glued to her thick, curvaceous frame. Bucket
naked. Oh my God...

"You are everything," I said as if I was in a
trance. "Turn around."

When she did my eyes took in every single inch
of her. My breath caught when my vision's focus landed
on that juicy ass. Finally, no clothes to obstruct my view.
I shook my head, trailed kisses down her back and then
got down on my knees. Without even thinking twice my
mouth was on her ass, sucking, kissing and licking those
cheeks.

"Uhhhh...mmm...Keys..." she moaned in
satisfaction.

Yup, I was about to eat the booty like groceries.
Besides, she smelled so damn good. The sweet aroma
that was permeating from her body was making me yearn

to taste every single inch of her. Even her pedicured toes were pretty as hell and they were going to get sucked on too. I was not going to leave any part of her sexy ass body untouched. Every single square inch of her frame was going to get some attention.

I gently spread her ass cheeks and got a good view of that fat ass pussy. My desire to release my hard dick and go ham on that shit was undeniable, but I kept it at bay. She needed to be loved and so I was going to show her that it was all about her. I wasn't going to be selfish like I was sure most men were.

I buried my face in it and used my tongue to tease and lick. My hands groped, caressed and massaged that soft ass as my warm, wet tongue teased her mercilessly.

"Fuck Keys…mmm…damn…" She sounded like she was out of breath already and I'd just gotten started.

Shit, I had to make myself stop, because I was enjoying it too much.

"Sit down," I instructed, not able to believe that I'd managed to still be fully dressed.

Her eyes were glazed over with unadulterated passion and I was ready to unleash it. She followed my instructions and sat down. I literally crawled over to her.

"Your body is amazin' Sen. For real ma."

"Thank you," she whispered as she reached out for me.

Those soft hands were on me again as she pulled my shirt over my head.

"I wanna feel your skin too," she said with her vulnerable eyes stuck on me.

My body trembled as she touched my chest and then my abs.

"I wanna taste you." My hands were on her thighs, ready to separate them and get a good look at the sweetness that dwelled between her thighs. "Open up ma."

She put her feet on the bench with her knees up and opened her legs wide. Shit, she was flexible.

"Ohh, I'm 'bout to enjoy this." I licked my lips.

A smile spread across her lips. "Me too."

I couldn't help but chuckle as I leaned over to kiss on her thighs. The fragrance of her pussy was doing exactly what it was supposed to do. The pheromones that she was letting off had me like a wild ass animal. I was in a feeding frenzy ready to feast on that shit.

"Mmm…" I moaned as my lips grazed against her smooth, waxed clean pussy.

Her hands were on the back of my neck and she was starting to apply pressure.

"Tired of me teasin' already?" I asked before blowing on her hard clitoris. Then I slowly slid my pointer and middle fingers inside of her tight, wetness.

"No…" Her breath caught when my fingers were lodged deep inside. "Ohh…"

I immediately felt the grip. Oh, hell yeah. That shit was so tight. Her eyes were stuck on my face as I licked my lips and stirred that pussy up. It was wet as fuck too, because I could clearly hear that shit popping.

"Damn, you got me wet as hell already," she whispered in disbelief.

"Shit, this ain't nothin' ma. Fuck that pool. This mufucka 'bout to be like the ocean."

I focused on the pretty, thick ass pussy that was in my face, front and center. Without wasting another second I was on it. I sucked and licked her clit before slurping it over and over with my long, thick expert tongue. Yeah, I loved eating pussy and I was A one at that shit too. That was evident by the way she had lifted her ass up and started grinding that pussy into my tongue.

"Uhhh...mmm...Keys...fuck!" Her mouth was opened as she stared down at me.

My eyes were on her challenging her to hold her orgasm back. I knew that she couldn't. Her body was jerking and her pussy was getting wetter.

"Mmm...you taste so good ma..."

Suddenly she made a face like she was in pain, but I knew what that face meant. She was about to cum. I could feel her pussy throbbing against my fingers and her clit was puffy as shit.

"Shiiiiiiiiit!!! Fuck...Keys..." Her pupils rolled back and then a peaceful look took over her gorgeous face. "Yesssssss...ohhhhh....mmmm...that feels...soooo...good."

She had stopped moving and just let me control her body. Her left ass cheek was in my left hand and my fingers on my right hand were pushing against her G-spot.

"Mmm…you taste so sweet ma…" I continued to slurp and lick her sensitivity until she exploded again.

Juices were trickling down my fingers into the palm of my hand as well as down my chin.

"I need some dick now. Damn." Her eyes were challenging me. "You can eat some pussy nigga. Shit."

I smiled cockily as I wiped her juices from my lips and then licked my fingers clean. Before I could blink she was unbuttoning my jeans.

"Damn ma, you ready huh?"

"Hell fuckin' yeah. I said gimme the dick!" There was a sexy, sly ass grin on her face.

As I leaned over to kiss her, she had those soft fingers locked around my hardness.

"Wow," she breathed as she released it from my boxers.

On hard I was at least nine inches, but my girth was what really had her attention. I had one of those thick dicks that hit every nook and cranny. Next thing I knew she had her hot mouth locked around my shit.

"Fuck!" Now my eyes were rolling back.

Her head was good, but I wanted some pussy.

"Damn ma, I wanna feel that juice box. Now." My fingers were inside of her again.

After stepping out of my jeans I positioned myself on top of her. Her fingers guided me to the heat of her entrance. The head of my dick felt the moisture before I even made it inside. My mind shouted for me to be smart and put on a condom, but damn…I wanted to feel her. I'd been wanting Sen in that way since I was fourteen years old.

My lips covered hers and we engaged in a feverish kiss that made us both shudder. I waited for her to stop and tell me to put on a condom, but she didn't. Instead that thang opened up for a nigga, but it was still a snug fit.

"Ahhhh…shit…" My initial reaction to the wet, warm sensation of suction made me shiver. Tears even came to a nigga's eyes because that shit felt so damn good.

"Mmm…Keys…" Her fingers massaged my back and ass as I grinded deep inside of her.

"Fuck Sen…what the hell…?" I squeezed my eyes closed and bit down on my bottom lip. Damn, I had to shut up before I told her I loved her fine ass.

She was so damn tight and deep that every stroke had my dick tingling like a mufucka. It was like my dick was made for her because that pussy hugged me like a glove. I squeezed her ass cheeks as she threw that shit back at me like we'd been fucking forever. The nerves were gone and it was nothing between us but pure pleasure.

"Damn right you were made for a nigga…" I whispered in her ear before sucking her earlobe.

After that I grabbed her foot and sucked on those pretty toes. When I was done with all ten of them she wrapped her legs around my waist and pulled me in like a vacuum seal. "Mmm…and you for me…"

* * *

We'd been going at it for hours and the sun was starting to set. As we lay there with our legs intertwined, my dick was still tingling from all of those nuts. I was definitely tired as hell, but I wanted some more. I'd never wanted to keep going up in a woman like that. Don't get me wrong, I'd had good pussy in the past. Sen though, she had me whipped already. Not once had I ever been whipped.

"Damn, you got my shit sore as hell, but why do I wanna keep right on making love to you?" She nibbled my neck and then came up for a kiss.

When I pulled away she sucked on my bottom lip gently.

"Cuz that shit felt so good. Damn, woman, you got me fucked up." I stared deep into her eyes and we were kissing again. "I don't think I've ever kissed this much."

"Hmm, well, it's a first time for everything. Are you hungry?"

My stomach was grumbling and it felt like my ribs were touching my back.

"Hell fuck yeah."

She laughed. "Hell fuck yeah?"

I nodded as I propped myself up to stare at her. "You're so fuckin' beautiful."

Her eyes casted down and her skin flushed.

"There you go blushin' again." I smiled at her and kissed her forehead, then the tip of her nose.

"You do that to me. No other man…well…other than my pops…has that effect on me." Her eyes were back on mine again and that time she didn't look away. "I…" she sighed. "I think I'm falling in love with you Keys. Do you think it's too soon to feel that way?"

"Nah baby girl, it's never too soon to feel that way when it's the right person. Hmm…" I pulled her into my arms. "I'm feelin' the same way you are."

We just sat there and enjoyed the feeling of finally knowing what completion was. She was the woman I'd always longed for and all I wanted to do was make her happy. The realness of the moment had kicked in and suddenly Mendosa and Trell popped up in my mind. I wondered if she was thinking about them too. Regardless, I wasn't going to let them spoil the moment. They'd be taken care of when the time came.

"Okay, let's go get something to eat," Sen's sweet, melodic voice greeted my ears like music.

"A'ight ma, but I'm cookin' for you. Just lead me to the kitchen."

She was literally glowing. "You don't have to tell me twice."

At that moment she looked happier than I'd seen her look since I'd laid eyes on her again.

* * *

After I had put it down in the kitchen we grubbed on fried chicken wings, brown rice and broccoli with cheese. Both of us had got the itis and fell asleep in the spooning position in one of the beds. When I opened my eyes the next morning it was after six am. It wasn't really like me to sleep late, so I popped up out of the bed.

As I recalled the night before my lips curved up into a big joker smile. Something on the pillow beside me caught my eye. It was an unopened toothbrush and a note.

Good morning sexy,
Here's a toothbrush for you. I figured I'd return the favor.
P.S. Yesterday was the best day of my life. You took me away without us even having to go anywhere.

Sen

My smile was even bigger after that. I'd put it down, but she had too. Damn, I could still feel her tight pussy wrapped around my dick like a rubber band. After washing my face and brushing my teeth I headed to the kitchen.

"Mmm, it's smells good in here." I walked up behind her, moved her hair out of the way and lightly kissed the back of her neck.

"Mmm…good morning handsome."

"Great morning baby," I said as I rubbed her bare butt cheek under the night shirt she had on. "No panties. Mmm, now my morning's even better."

"Don't start nothing. I whipped up these omelets and you're gonna eat."

"I ain't say I wasn't gonna eat ma," I teased.

She giggled and turned around to kiss me.

"Turn the stove off." I narrowed my eyes at her attempting to make my sexy face.

"No," she protested with a smile and turned back around. "I'm almost done."

I pressed my hardness into her back. She swatted me away playfully.

"Go sit down Keys."

"Nope." My hands were under her shirt pinching her nipples just as she removed the omelet from the pan and put it on a plate. "Turn the stove off."

When she turned around that time she wasn't smiling anymore.

"You're something else…"

I reached over and turned the stove off before moving the pan to a cool burner. Then I picked her up and sat her down on top of the counter.

"Now, it's time to eat," I said licking my lips as I spread her thick, luscious thighs apart.

* * *

A nigga had business to handle, so I was headed back to the crib. I had to go to campus and register for my Fall classes, so I needed to take a quick shower and throw on some clothes. After that it was time to hit the streets and make some money. Damn, I wished I could actually take Sen out and spend some on her. For the time being we had to keep our relationship on the low.

She'd decided to go back to her father's crib for a little while. I'd promised her that I would go back to the spot with her so that she wouldn't have to be alone. I also decided to follow her and then I'd head home once I was sure that she was safely at Mendosa's.

My mind was on all of that good loving the night before and that morning. We'd had another heated session before finally eating the breakfast she'd cooked. I almost didn't see the dark colored car that was coming down a side road. We weren't that far from the house and the street was damn near empty. I guess I noticed the car because it was approaching at an unusually high speed.

Pop! Pop! Pop!

It sounded like firecrackers at first, but it soon registered that what I'd heard were gunshots. I focused on Sen's car and watched as it spun out of control in front of me. As it ventured into the grass, I focused on the other car and noticed that it had come to a complete halt on the side of the road. I hit the brake and stopped right there in the middle of the road before grabbing my gun from the arm rest.

When I got out of the car a tall, dark skinned man in a black suit was walking toward Sen's car. I hadn't even seen her hit the tree and all I could do was hope that she wasn't hurt or dead. Had he shot her and if so why? I had no idea who that nigga was. It was like he didn't even know I was there, or he didn't care as I made my way over to him.

Without hesitation I pointed my gun and he turned around. Just as he lifted his weapon I squeezed the trigger.

Pow! Pow! Pow!

He had left off two rounds.

Pop! Pop!

I managed to duck his shots, but one of my bullets hit his shoulder and the other two hit him in the abdomen. Good, none of my bullets were wasted. He was stunned as he dropped his gun and hit the ground. When I got closer to him I looked around to make sure that nobody was coming. I was so glad that it was early as hell and we were on a country road. The thing was I had to be careful to get out of there before somebody did drive up. I didn't know if he was dead, so I let off one more round in his head.

Pow!

My heart was beating so fast and I was sweating hard as shit by the time I made it to Sen's car. Her head was resting on the steering wheel and her eyes were closed. The first thing I did was check her for a pulse. It was strong, so that meant she was still alive. I lifted her head and then checked her body for blood or bullet wounds. It was a good thing I didn't see any. I unbuckled her seat belt and quickly pulled her out of the car along with her purse. Putting her limp body over my shoulder, I rushed to my car, put her in the passenger seat and buckled her in.

"Sen, baby…can you hear me?" I asked once I was behind the wheel.

There was no time to waste, so I pulled off and headed to my crib. My first thought was to take her to the hospital, but the only injury she had was a slight bruise on her head from what I could see. Obviously the gunman's bullet had simply shot her tires out and made her lose control of the car.

"Mmm…" she let out a low moan and started moving around in the seat.

"Sen…baby…you okay?"

Chapter 9

Jasenia
Miami, Fla
2 months ago

"What, what do you mean?" I asked my mother as she stared at me with a blank expression on her face.

"He wants you sweetheart and I need you to cooperate," she said with her hand on my shoulder.

I was sitting at my vanity doing my make up for what I thought was a business dinner with my mom and an associate of hers. The plan was to extend her clientele.

Over the past few years I'd done what she asked and recruited some of the best money makers for her. The guilt that I felt over ruining the lives of women who once had dreams and goals was trumped by how much money I was making. My father gave me anything I wanted, but extra was always good. Suddenly, at that moment none of that shit seemed to be worth it.

I made eye contact with my mother in the mirror. "So, you told him that I wasn't for sale right?" Although I asked, I knew better.

There was no limit to what that woman would do and at that point I was more than disgusted with her. If I'd never wanted to hurt her before I did then.

She looked away and rubbed her hands together while attempting to make the lewd proposal sound good.

"Jasenia, c'mon, woman up. It's not like you ain't never fucked for money before."

"You never cease to amaze me! Are you serious? You really think I'm gonna go fuck this dude so that you can do business with him?"

"Uh, yeah! What if your father really cuts us off like he's been threatening to do? Huh? What are we going to do then?" Her eyes were wide and she looked like a crazed maniac as she spoke.

"My father will never cut me off. Just because he's tired of taking care of your greedy ass doesn't mean that he's tired of taking care of me!" I shot back.

It was clear to see that my words had fucked with her. "You're gonna stop talking to me like that bitch! I'm your mother! Shit! I should've aborted your worthless ass! All you've ever been is a fucking burden to me!"

When she grabbed my hair and pulled me out of the chair I was sitting in, I was stunned. She'd always talked shit, but never had she actually put her hands on me. I swung my fists above my head as best I could and landed a few punches to her face. She let me go huffing and puffing like we'd been boxing for twelve rounds.

"I hate you!" I screamed enraged with anger. "I'm not going anywhere and I'm not fucking anybody for you to come up!"

With that said I grabbed my cellphone to call my father. I had to tell him what my mother was trying to make me do and the fact that she had actually assaulted me. At that point I didn't care if he killed her trifling ass. She'd never been a real mother to me anyway.

"What the fuck are you doing?" She asked.

"Calling my father. He needs to know the truth about you!"

She gave me a cold look as she snatched the phone from my hand.

"What about him knowing the truth about you? If you don't do what the fuck I told you to do I'll tell your precious daddy about the abortion you had last year."

The menacing tone of her voice and the fury in her eyes told me that she would.

I rolled my eyes at her in defiance. "I don't give a fuck. I'll just deny it."

"Don't forget that I paid for it, so I have the proof. Ha! Oh and how about the time he thought you were in Paris, but you were in rehab for three months."

A few months after the abortion I'd checked myself into rehab due to my addiction to Oxycontin and Xanax. I'd been off them ever since. Of course I didn't want my father to find out about that. The thought infuriated me.

"You're so childish and petty!" I wanted to really hurt that bitch. "I wish you weren't my mother!"

"Well, I wish you weren't my daughter, but what's done is done right! No need to cry over spilled milk." Her eyes were gauging my face for a reaction to her words.

Did my mother just refer to my birth as spilled milk? Wow. Shit, it didn't even hurt anymore. I guess I couldn't miss what I never had; a mother's love.

All I could do was shake my head as I sighed. I didn't want my father to know about the abortion I'd had, nor my stint in rehab. He would be so disappointed in me. For the time being I was going to go along with that twisted shit, but I wasn't going to fuck anybody. Somehow, someway, I was going to find a way out of it.

"I can't believe you!" I hissed. "Do you feel anything for the child you pushed out of your pussy? That's why I got that damn abortion! I don't wanna be a fucked up ass mother like you!"

She rolled her eyes and then clapped her hands like I was putting on an act.

"What a great performance Sen. You've always been a great actress baby girl. Whatever you have to do for attention. That's how you always got to your father. He was always weak for your ass. Of course I feel something for you. You're mine. The thing is, I've never felt connected with you. Not even when you were a baby. You're definitely your father's child, but that's beside the point right now."

Was that bitch really trying to sweet talk me after she'd just attacked me? My father was right, she was a mental case for real. It was just a matter of time before her behavior got her committed. If she put her hands on me again, I was going to fuck her ass up like she was some hoe in the streets.

"Okay," I said softly figuring that letting her think I was obliging would be best at the moment. "Just leave please so I can finish getting dressed."

"Alright baby girl. Wear that sexy, red Tom Ford dress. He'd love that."

There was a mad ass look on my face, but I was trying my best to throw her off.

"Oh, baby girl relax. It'll only be a couple days," my mother added that bit of information at the very last minute.

It was another bombshell she'd dropped, just like informing me that I was supposedly sleeping with a client for her.

"Two days? You gotta be fucking kidding me. I can't with you!" I stumped off toward the bathroom.

"It's okay Sen. You're getting half a million dollars out of the deal!"

"No, you're getting half a million dollars out of the deal. I might just get ten percent of that! What you're asking me to do is not okay! Fuck you...mother!" I slammed the bathroom door, sat down on the toilet and cried my eyes out.

Less than two hours later I was in a luxurious suite at the Ritz Carlton Hotel with a strange, older man. He was about 5'10 with a slim build and graying hair. It wasn't that he was bad looking, but I just wasn't into having sex with men that I wasn't physically attracted to for money. That just wasn't my thing. I couldn't believe *that my mother was treating me like I was one of her hoes.*

"Wow, you're so...beautiful. I wanted you from the first moment I saw you. When Missy told me that you were her daughter I didn't think she'd let me be with you, but..." His voice trailed off when he noticed the look in my eyes. "It's okay. I won't hurt you. Well, not on purpose."

I shivered. His name was Will according to him and my mom told me that he was a human trafficker. He ran a prostitution ring that had clientele all over the world. My mother wanted to tap into that arena and actually auction off some of her girls for Will's "business". The thing was Will didn't trust her. He claimed that if she'd sacrifice me, that was the only way to gain his trust to do business. My mother saw dollar signs and I saw red.

I wasn't nervous, but I was anxious to get the hell up out of there. Two days were too damn long to be stuck with a man I didn't know or particularly like. He took women all over the world and profited from them having sex. True, my mother profited from women having sex, but it was their choice. From what I knew about Will, most of his prostitutes didn't consent. Most had been kidnapped and some were underage. After they captured them they'd get them addicted to drugs to keep them complacent.

"I'm fine," I said simply as my mind worked on a way for me to make a break for it.

It seemed that I could simply run up out of there, but something told me that he wasn't going to let his investment just sneak away. Something told me that he was going to keep a close eye on me.

"Do you want a drink?" He asked hopefully. "Maybe it'll loosen you up." His chestnut colored skin was pretty smooth for his age, but his small, dark, sly eyes made him look evil.

His way of talking was sweet for the moment, but I was sure that his true side would come out eventually. We were all the way on the twelfth floor, so it wasn't like I could just leave through the window. Damnit, I wasn't trying to fuck that old ass man for any amount of money. My thoughts drifted to my father and how he would be disappointed in me. Then I thought about Trell and what he would do if he knew about what I was doing.

Instead of pissing him off by refusing I went ahead and accepted although I didn't plan to drink it. "Sure, a drink would be fine."

I flashed him a smile and he smiled back before getting up. He had his back to me, so I was able to tuck my slim, butterfly knife in the waistband of my thong before he turned around.

"Vodka or cognac?" He asked.

The smile was plastered on my face. "Vodka. Please add some juice."

He turned around again and I heard the sound of ice clinking in the glass. What if he planned to drug me and take advantage of me? Just because he seemed pleased by my mere presence, I knew that sex was coming. There was no way I was going through with that shit.

After making our drinks he sat back down next to me and passed me a glass.

"I prefer cognac," he said.

I nodded knowing that I'd asked for vodka because it was see through. After pretending to take a sip, I sat the glass down on the table.

"So Will, tell me a little bit about yourself." I was still smiling all hard, but in all actuality I wanted to bolt for the door.

"Well, I'm fifty six years young and I got a lot of fuckin' money. That's all that matters."

I went along with his attempt to seduce me with his funds. "Shit, you're right about that." After licking my lips, I acted like I was taking another sip of the drink he'd made.

His eyes were glued on me. "Mmm mmm mmm. I'on wanna waste no mo' time."

"We got all weekend right?" I asked hoping he'd give me more time to figure out my escape.

"Yeah, but the plan is to use every minute wisely. Shit, I got you and I'm tryna take advantage." The way he was looking at me was like a lion stalking his prey.

"Hmm, well...What do you have in mind?" I tried to act sexy and seductive, but I really wanted to throw up in my mouth.

His cologne was too damn strong and he wasn't my cup of tea in the first place. If only I had the heart to confess who I really was to my father, I wouldn't be in the fucked up ass position that I was in.

Will grabbed my hand and pulled me up from my seat. "C'mon love. Let's go in the bedroom."

My nerves were really fucked up at that point and I hoped he wouldn't be able to see the bulge of the knife in the tight dress I had on. Damn! What the fuck was I going to do? Shit was happening too damn fast.

"Okay, uhhh...I can't lie...I'm nervous. My mom may have left out the fact that I'm not used to doing this. Uhhh, a shower always relaxes me. You mind if I take one first?" I tried to look and sound as innocent as possible.

It must've worked because he nodded as he smiled from ear to ear. "Hell yeah. You can do whatever you wanna do. As a matter of fact, a shower would be perfect. I'll join you."

My heart sank. Shit, that wasn't part of the plan. The whole point of the shower was for me to come up with something. Damnit!

"Okay," I said reluctantly. "I'm a little bashful, so you go in the bathroom and get the shower ready while I get undressed."

He shook his head. "Oh no...I'm not letting you out of my sight. I already paid your mama and I'on need you slippin' out of here 'cause you got second thoughts.

Don't think you can get away with some bullshit. My niggas know where I'm at and who I'm with."

I gulped. "I wasn't plannin' on doing anything."

"Okay, c'mon. I'll get in the shower while you undress in the bathroom if it makes you feel better."

That didn't really make me feel any better, but I followed him anyway. While he undressed I tried my best not to show how much he was really repulsing me by keeping a seductive look on my face. He was buying that fake shit. As a matter of fact he was eating it up.

"You like what you see gorgeous?" He asked just as he dropped his drawers.

His wrinkled dick was all shriveled up and short. I almost laughed out loud, but I held it in. At least if I went along with having sex with him it wouldn't hurt. For some reason I looked around the bedroom. There were handcuffs, a whip, chains, and all types of shit laid out on the bed.

What the fuck was that fool thinking? He was a sexual deviant and that became painfully obvious. Oh, he was one of those muthafuckas. He couldn't hurt a bitch with his little dick, so he had to hurt women in other ways. After seeing that shit I knew what I had to do. There was no way he was doing the crazy, freaky ass shit that he was planning for me. Hell nah. Without giving him a clue about what I was thinking, I pretended that the items on the bed didn't bother me one bit.

He was butt naked as I followed him into the bathroom.

"I can't wait to get my hands on yo' fine ass I'm gon' do all types of shit to you. Hmm, you just don't know. I can't wait to get all up in that young pussy. I know it's good. Mmm!" There was a huge, toothy smile on his face and his beer belly moved as he chuckled.

Eww, his body was fucking disgusting as hell and when he started stroking his limp dick I wanted to disappear. When he turned around to turn the shower on I was relieved. I quickly moved the knife to the back of my thong. He turned around and stared me down again.

"Okay, I'm 'bout to get in, so go ahead and get undressed."

"A'ight." My smile had to be enticing him because he didn't press the issue as he stepped in the shower.

I pulled my dress over my head and he watched me attentively.

"You are perfect..." He was literally drooling and my mind was racing trying to come up with something.

It was to no avail. There was only one way out. I was not going to let him violate me. There was no fucking way.

"Thank you." I was seducing him with my eyes as I removed my push up bra.

His tongue was hanging out like a panting dog and it was hard for me to keep up my sexy, willing to fuck *routine. It was only a matter of time before my true feelings started seething.*

For a split second he turned away to lather up and I removed my thong while holding the knife in my right hand. He didn't notice as I stepped in the shower behind him. I was surprised that he kept his back to me and continued to wash himself. Damn, that shit was going to be easier than I thought and I had to act fast.

Without even giving him a clue of what I was doing, I flipped the knife so that the handles were down and the blade was up. The cascading water masked the sound and he was oblivious. With a flick of my wrist the blade was in his back. I swiftly pulled it out and stabbed again and again and again. The sight of his blood really unleashed the beast inside of me. As I stabbed him over and over I saw my mother's face. The truth was, I really wanted to put the blade of that knife in her, but I couldn't. Because of that, I was going to take my vengeance out on him. By the time I was finished he was lying on his back, his body was still and the crimson blood was running down the drain with the water.

There were so many stab wounds in his body and I knew that he was dead. I allowed the water to wash the remnants of blood from my naked body and stepped out of the shower. I removed the knife from his neck and rinsed it off in the water. Instead of turning it off, I just let the shower run. I figured he'd just bleed out over time.

After drying off, I grabbed my purse and put my knife inside. After I got dressed I went to check on Will again. He was definitely a goner and I was so damn glad.

I grabbed the glass that I had drank out of and stashed it in my purse too. After that I wiped down anything that could've had my finger prints on it. Not only was that nigga not going to take advantage of me, but he'd never take advantage of anybody else again. That shit felt damn good.

* * *

"Arrrghhhhhhh!!" I screamed out as I opened my eyes. Keys was standing over me. The feeling of something cold on my forehead caught my attention. It must've been ice, so I relaxed. At first I thought it was a gun.

"Sen, baby, you're okay. You're with me ma." He said with genuine concern in his eyes.

At the moment I didn't feel any pain and I couldn't remember anything past leaving McDonough to drive to my father's house. Of course the memory of our love making was vivid as hell.

"Where am I?" I looked around at my surroundings.

"At my spot," he said. "You don't remember what happened?"

"No, what happened? All I remember is…" I grinned slyly. "And then I was driving to my father's…Ohhh…" The memories suddenly came flooding in. "Shit, the man..."

"I killed him," Keys disclosed with a look of vengeance in his eyes. "He was…he was after you. Why would somebody be after you Sen? You think it got something to do with Trell?"

I shook my head. "No…it's…I…" Fuck, how could I tell him that I'd killed a very dangerous man and now his criminal organization was after me?

It wasn't Trell sending anybody after me. It was Will's people and I knew it. That was who me and my mother had been running from and they'd finally found me. Maybe I should've gone to Puerto-Rico with her, but I couldn't stand to be in the same space as her for too long. I just knew that they wouldn't find me, but going to Georgia may not have been the best idea.

"Trell's the least of my worries…Thank you for…killing him and saving my life."

"I'm just glad I was there baby. I thought you'd been shot." The stress on his face showed that he really gave a shit about me. "What the fuck Sen?"

If only he knew how much I had longed for somebody to really care. I knew that my father cared, but for some reason that wasn't enough.

"Don't judge me…" I could feel the pain in my head all of a sudden.

"It's too late for that. I already got feelings for you." His eyes glimmered with understanding and I could tell that he adored me.

Without a second thought I filled him in on my mother's attempt to sell my body for her own gain. When I told him the details of the murder his face didn't change. Once it was all out I felt like I'd purged my guilt and for some reason, although somebody was trying to kill me, I felt a little better.

"Oh shit Sen, this shit's really serious ma. You have to tell Men…"

"No! Are you serious Keys? Do you hear yourself? He'll kill me!"

He shook his head as he kissed my hand. "No he won't. He loves you more than anything and he can help. Why are you so afraid to tell him the truth?"

"Because, he's the only person who really gives a shit about me. I don't want him to hate me. If he hates me I have nobody."

Keys shook his head vigorously. "No, that's not true. I really give a shit about you. I love you. You got me and you always will."

My heart melted instantly. "I love you too Keys." Then my next thought ruined the moment. "Oh shit. My car…It's in my father's name and it's at a murder scene!"

"I took care of that already baby. Don't worry. I called Dame and he handled it. Guess that nigga's good for something. That's such a deserted road that when he got there the body was still in the same place. It's a good thing it's like a ditch there and even if a car passed by they may have missed the body, but eventually someone would've been suspicious about his car on the side of the road and your car smashed into a tree. Now it's a matter of getting rid of the people who are after you. Wow." He sighed. "So not only is Trell an issue, but it seems I got my work cut out for me to keep you alive ma."

I felt like shit for getting him involved in my mess. The tears formed against my will again. "I'm so sorry Keys…"

"Shhhh…" He ran his fingers through my hair and held me close. "No need to apologize. I gotcha ma and I ain't lettin' nothin' happen to you."

"Thank you Keys." I tried to calm down and get my thoughts together. "If it wasn't for you I'd be dead."

"Like I said, I got you. That's my word. How does your head feel? I was gonna take you to the hospital, but…"

"No, I'm fine. No hospitals. When they figure out that their hit man is dead and didn't do the job I'm sure they're gonna come after me again. I have to call my mom. Shit, I should've went with her to Puerto-Rico."

"I know shit's fucked up ma, but if you had gone to Puerto-Rico, *we* wouldn't be happening."

I leaned over and kissed him. "You're right. I guess it's bittersweet."

"Well, go ahead and call your mom. I'll give you a minute. Make sure you call Mendosa too and let him know that you're okay. You're not leavin' though. You're stayin' here until we figure shit out. Obviously whoever's after you knows about the spot in McDonough."

I nodded in agreement. "Okay, but I need some…"

"Make a list and I'll get whatever you need. If you want I'll go to your condo and pick up some clothes for you too," he stated matter of factly and I couldn't help but feel taken care of. It felt good.

"Thank you again Keys."

He nodded and left the room.

Anxiety kicked in as I dialed my mother's number. As much as I hated her, I still didn't want anything to happen to her. I tapped my foot on the floor as the phone rang. Finally after five rings she answered.

"Sen?"

"Hey, yeah, it's me."

"You okay? I had an awful dream…"

"I'm fine." The bitch actually sounded like she gave a fuck, which was a first. "Uh, they're after me." I filled her in as best I could over the phone.

There was silence on the other line for a while. All that did was give me time to think back. After I murdered Will I went straight to my mother and told her. At first she brushed it off although she was angry at me. According to her everything would be fine. That was until two weeks later when one of her hoes was found murdered in a hotel room in the shower with multiple stab wounds. It was like a copycat had duplicated the murder that I'd committed. Will's murder had been all over the news, so we brushed that off too.

Less than a week later another one of my mother's hoes was found killed in the same manner, but a note was left behind that time. The media hadn't leaked what the letter said, but that was the first time we realized that we were really in danger. A note arrived at our home the next day.

We know what happened and you will pay with your lives.

That was all that it said. After that it didn't take long for me and my mother to flee. Obviously Will's organization was fucking with us big time. They could've got to us, but it was more satisfying to play a cat and mouse game.

"Oh my God,' my mother finally muttered. "It's only a matter of time before they come for me too. Damnit, why didn't you just fuck the man Sen! "

Wow. I rolled my eyes. So, the one second that I felt like she genuinely gave a damn was bullshit. I should've known. She hadn't even asked me what had happened, or if I was okay. That heifer was only concerned about herself. Instead of reacting, I decided to get off the phone before I cussed her out. I was back to not giving a fuck about her selfish ass.

"I just thought I'd let you know. I survived this time, but I don't know what'll happen if they send someone else. Bye...mother." My voice dripped with sarcasm, but she didn't seem to notice.

"Okay. Look, please, don't tell your father," she pleaded. "We are going to make it through this honey."

I rolled my eyes. "Yeah whatever. How can he protect me if he doesn't even know that I'm in danger? Just be careful mother. Bye."

Before she could respond, I ended the call.

After that I called my father and made up some lie about going to see Nadia in Miami for a couple days. I saw that Trell was blowing my phone up, so I called him next. All I had to do was pacify him a little bit and assure him that I wasn't going to renege on him.

"Damn bitch, when you comin' back?" He asked harshly. "I ain't got time to be sittin' here tryna figure out where yo' head at. If you cross me I'm killin' yo' whole fuckin' family. Know that shit! Get yo' ass back to Atlanta!"

"Calm down Trell." I sighed and rolled my eyes. "You don't have to worry. You'll get your part of the deal if you're really gonna leave me and my father alone after you get what you want. Just make sure the word doesn't get out that I helped you. My father would never forgive me."

"I'on give a fuck about that shit bitch! Just get yo' ass back here before I come to Miami to find yo' ass!"

"Ok. I'll be back day after tomorrow. Then I'll have a talk with my father to find out that information for you."

"Just make sure you be here and do what the fuck I told you to do. I'll hit you in the mornin' and answer your fuckin' phone!"

With that said he hung up in my ear. If he went to Miami looking for me that would be just fine. As long as he was nowhere near me I was okay.

Keys came back into the room a few minutes later with an ink pen and a notepad.

"Here you go. Just write down what you need and gimme the key to your spot."

I looked up at him. "You sure you wanna go to my place? What if that nigga Trell's lurking around or what if Will's people sent someone to finish the job already?"

My nerves were all fucked up, but Keys played it cool. "I ain't worried about none of that shawty. I would go buy you a whole new wardrobe, but time is of the essence. I know that you're used to nice things and you ain't even tryna lounge up in here in bullshit. I gotta handle some business at Clark and then I gotta make a run to my pops to pick up some shit. If it makes you feel any better I'll talk to you the whole time I'm there."

I nodded. "Okay."

After I finished my list he gave me a sweet kiss and left. Suddenly my nerves were kicking in again and my head was killing me. I'd taken a couple Ibuprofens and tried to eat a sandwich that Keys had made, but I had no appetite. My life seemed to be falling apart and the worst part was the fact that my future wasn't looking as bright as it used to. There would be no degree for me anytime soon. Once I got involved in my mother's illegal business ventures I fell off when it came to school. Just last month I was sent a letter informing me that I'd been withdrawn from the University and I had lost my scholarship. Why I'd waited until my senior year to do that, I'd never know. I still hadn't told my father about it.

He'd be so disappointed. I didn't even know if I wanted to tell Keys. If I did what would he see in me? I was just ruined all the way around.

The sound of the doorbell interrupted my pity party and sent me into an instant panic. Something told me to just stay put, but then something else told me to at least look out of the peep hole. At least I could tell Keys what his visitor looked like. From what I knew he wasn't expecting anybody. As I made it toward the door my heart was beating erratically against my rib cage.

There some chick was standing there. Hmm, what if they'd sent some unsuspecting looking woman to off me. It was mighty funny that she'd shown up right after Keys left. Then I had a feeling that she was there for Keys. Shit, I was bored, so why not fuck with her? Suddenly a voice told me not to open the door. What if I was right the first time?

"Keys! Keys! Are you in there?" She called out with desperation in her voice. "Open the door! I really need to talk to you!"

A smile crept up on my face as I looked down at myself. I was wearing one of his tee shirts, so of course it was obvious that we had an intimate relationship. So, my first thought wasn't correct. She *was* there for Keys. Oh yeah, it was time to have some fun with old girl. I needed to take my grief out on somebody.

Without hesitation, I swung the door open and let her get an eye full. I had a bruise on my head, but I'd swept my hair over it. She didn't need to be trying to figure out what had happened. Knot on my head or not, I would still whoop that hoe's ass if I had to.

"You lookin' for Keys?" I asked.

There was a stunned look on her face, but she suddenly snapped out of it. "Uh, yeah, is he here?"

"Nah. Who're you?" As I looked her up and down she was assessing me too.

She was cute, but not as fine as me. Yeah, I was conceited in the midst of some fucked up shit, but that was just me.

"Who the fuck are you?" Her face was all screwed up as she asked.

"That's really irrelevant being that I'm standing here and you're standing there." I pointed.

She sucked her teeth and shook her head. "Well, who are you to Keys?"

"Who the fuck are you to Keys?" I sized her up for the fight.

Damn, I had so much pent up anger inside of me that I needed a punching bag. That bitch would do just fine. I was ready to pound her pretty face for coming to see my man. After she'd seen me come to the door she should've just turned her thirsty ass around.

She rolled her eyes. "Look. I don't have time for these childish ass games. Are you fucking him or not?

"Well, since you asked bitch, hell yeah I'm fucking him. What is it to you?"

Tears filled her eyes and spilled down her cheeks. "For...for how long?" She swiped them away as she asked.

I shook my head at that weak ass bitch. "What the fuck you crying for? Damn. How long we've been fucking doesn't matter. Just know that he's mine now."

That bitch lunged for me and I literally drug her inside of the apartment by her hair, closed the door with my foot so there'd be no witnesses and whooped her ass.

"Bitch!" She screamed. "Get the fuck off me."

"Fuck you hoe! I'm gon' kill you!" All I saw was red and I wanted to hurt her bad.

Like always when I went into a rage, I envisioned myself beating my mother into a pulp instead. I was sitting on top of that chick going ham as my fists kept connecting with her face. When I started slamming her head into the floor I realized that I was going too far. My eyes were on her face and the sight of blood took me back to what happened to Will. Also, the fact that she wasn't fighting back made me contain myself. Shit, I didn't want another body on my hands unless it was Trell's.

She was groaning, which let me know that she was still alive. I stood up and pulled her up from the floor. At first she seemed to be a little woozy, but she was staring straight at me with wide eyes.

"You psychotic ass bitch," she spat with blood pouring from her mouth.

"Well, you asked for it bitch! You swung at me first. Be careful who you try to fight. Now get the fuck outta her before I murk yo' ass!"

The fear in her eyes said it all as she turned to leave. I didn't know if she was going to report me to the police and at that point I didn't give a shit. If I got locked up I'd be safe from Trell and Will's goons for a little while. Shit, then I wouldn't have to explain the fucked up shit I'd done to my father. I'd rather tell him that I beat some hoe's ass. Then again, that wouldn't work, because my pops would be at the jail to bail me out asap.

That bitch bolted for the door, opened it and slammed it on her way out. I'd never in my life fought somebody and they ran for their damn life afterwards. I didn't even get the hoe's name. Keys would probably be mad at me. I was sure that she would call and tell him about what had happened.

All of a sudden a dizzy spell took over me and I slowly made my way over to the sofa. I guess after my head injury that little fight had made me over exert myself. Instead of over thinking shit, I decided to try to relax and turned on the television. Keys was going to call soon and I had some questions for his ass. The first two were, who the hell was that bitch and why was she crying and ready to fight over him? That nigga had some explaining to do.

Chapter 10

Keenyn

"Fuck you doin' shawty?" I asked when Sen answered the phone.

"She swung at me first! Who the fuck is that bitch anyway?" She asked defensively.

I was pulling into a parking spot at Clark when a text from Elena came through. Her calls were blocked of course, so we hadn't actually talked. If her texts were blocked too, I wouldn't have known what had gone down.

Elena: That bitch at ur crib jumped on me and shit. U need to control ur hoes.

Me: Nah ma u need to stop poppin up at my spot. I told u I'm done wit ur ass.

She'd sent a few more texts, but I hadn't read them because I immediately called Sen.

"Her name's Elena. She's my ex. Come to find out she had a man the entire time." I explained the situation to her. "You can't be gettin' in no more shit yo'. It's enough goin' on already.

She sighed heavily. "I'm sorry Keys. Like I said, she swung first. I was just defending myself."

"You shouldn't have opened the door. What if she was there to…?"

She cut me off. "I thought about that too, but she called your name…so."

"Look, don't open the door for nobody else okay. I'll be there in a little while." I was a little irritated, but something about her beating Elena's ass turned me on.

"Okay," she said. "Don't be mad at me."

"I ain't mad. I just want you to stay outta trouble ma. Straight up."

"K. See you when you get here."

"A'ight."

"I love you Keys."

"Love you back baby."

I hung up knowing that I would have to convince Elena not to press charges. The only thing working in Sen's favor was the fact that Elena popped up at my spot and started the confrontation with her. I decided to go ahead and read her other text messages.

Elena: I should get that bitch locked up. I been tryin to call u because I found out that I'm pregnant. Since I got no answer I wanted to tell you in person. I hope my baby's ok after that dumb hoe attacked me.

Fuck! I was stunned as hell, but it was a chance that it wasn't mine. Besides, I didn't believe her ass anyway. I'd always used condoms and she claimed to be on the pill.

Me: That's all fine and dandy. I'll hear from you after you test yo' nigga. Let me know.

Elena: What the fuck ever. It's urs.

Me: First of all I don't give a fuck what u sayin. U was fuckin me and that nigga. Do what u feel. Either way I'm done wit ur ass. Now don't call or text me again unless u ready to get a DNA test.

She sent a picture message after that of a positive pregnancy test. It didn't even matter to me. That shit could've came from anywhere. Instead of responding I decided to let time do what it did best, prove the damn truth. If she was really pregnant and the child was mine, I would take care of it. I wasn't going to be forced to be with a woman I didn't want to be with though. Hell nah.

I finally got out of my car and headed toward what I knew was going to be a long line. At first I was going to register online, but I had to visit my advisor anyway. I was actually working toward being a college educated black man. That was proof that you didn't always have to be a product of your environment. Shit, all I knew were drug dealers and most of them hadn't made it past the tenth grade.

The off the wall shit that was going on with Sen had me reevaluating my life. Maybe I should really consider a career if I made it out of "Operation Protect Sen" alive. A voice rang inside of my head telling me to leave the drug game alone and go legit. Then again…I loved fast, easy money.

* * *

After running around to get everything that Sen needed, I made the trip to her condo to get her clothes and personal items. I put in the code and waited for the gate to open. While proceeding, I took a quick look around, but didn't notice anything out of the ordinary. Like I had promised her, we talked the entire time.

Instead of going to my father's afterwards to get the work, I decided to put it off until later. Of course Dame held the favor he'd just done for me over my head, so I agreed to go ahead and fuck with those niggas he'd been telling me about. The transaction would be going down the next day. It was best for me to just get back to Sen and try to smooth over the bullshit that had gone down with Elena.

* * *

"Come on ma. You can't sit here and act like you surprised that I was fuckin' somebody before you. Damn. I told you the truth about ol' girl. Why the fuck you trippin'?" Were we having our first argument?

Shit, we hadn't actually said that we were a couple out of our mouths, but that shit was inevitable. There was something between us and it was deeper than great sex.

"I ain't trippin'. I just...I just wanna know if you still got feelings for her. I mean, like you said, you found out the truth about her the day before we saw each other again. How do you feel about her?"

Was she really being insecure? Did she not know how incredible she was? Shit, I'd loved her my whole life. I finally had her and she thought I still wanted Elena. All I could do was put my head in my hand.

I sighed. "I don't give a fuck about her if that's what you wanna know. I won't lie and say that I didn't feel something for her at first. That's over now. Don't question that. I love you Sen. Always have." It was hard to leave out the fact that Elena claimed to be pregnant, but it wasn't the right time to reveal that bit of information.

"And you know that I love you too. I'm sorry Keys. I just…I don't wanna lose you."

I softly kissed the bump on her head. The swelling was going down, but the bruise was getting darker. "You ain't gonna lose me ma. Calm down."

In the back of my mind I wondered about her feelings for Trell. Of course it was clear that his change in demeanor and his threats had her frightened, but how did she feel about him at first? Was she one of those women who preferred men like Trell and Dame over men like me? I mean, I was probably fifty percent bad boy, but my heart was good. When it came to women, I didn't believe in blatantly disrespecting, or abusing them.

Truth be told, I wasn't perfect by far, but I didn't get any pleasure out of hurting someone who cared about me. Now, hurting a fuck nigga who wanted to sabotage me was a different story. When it came to the plan to murk Trell, I wondered where her head was at.

"In case you're wondering, I never loved Trell." Her voice was low and her soft lips were on my neck.

Damn, she had an uncanny way of knowing exactly what I was thinking. That shit was kind of scary, but it was intriguing at the same time. When it came to Sen, I was bewitched. I was under her spell and there wasn't shit that I could do about it. I knew that being with her put my life in danger, but I didn't care. All I really gave a shit about was keeping her out of harm's way. Not knowing if I was going to live the next day didn't even fuck with me, as long as I could be with her for the moment.

"I'on understand what you ever saw in that nigga in the first place."

"Me either, now that I think about it. Like I said before, the fact that I knew him when we were kids seemed to make me want to trust him. I shouldn't have though." She moved and leaned against the pillow at the far end of the sofa. After she repositioned herself, she put her feet in my lap.

"I thought about it and I know that I said I was gonna keep Dame out of it at first, but maybe he can help. We gotta get this shit over wit' ma. Ain't no need to drag it along for too long. So, we gon' come up wit' some shit when I meet wit' him tomorrow."

She nodded. "I don't really wanna talk about that right now babe."

"Okay," I agreed.

I watched her face as she reached for something on the end table. Next thing I knew, I smelled the sweet aroma of some Ganja. A smile snuck up on my face as I watched her puff on the blunt. Damn, she could roll up. It was something about a woman who could cook and roll a blunt. Not only that, but her pussy and head were both A one. Hell yeah, ma was marriage material.

"A biochemist that can roll a blunt…" I shook my head.

"Well, you know…" She giggled and blew O's out of her mouth before passing the blunt to me.

"I got the best of both worlds wit' you," I said as I took a hit of the blunt.

"Meaning?" She asked although she already knew what I meant.

"I got a classy, hood ass chick who knows how to act like a lady, but thinks like a boss. Once all of this shit is over, we gon' be a power couple ma. It ain't no tellin' what we gon' do. Shit, we can conquer the world." I smiled all big at her as I passed the blunt back.

"Damn." She shook her head. "You're one fine ass nigga yo'. For real."

I massaged her foot and she sat up to give me a kiss.

"That's a compliment comin' from a woman who looks as good as you."

"Stop," she said playfully.

We both laughed.

"I'm glad you can laugh despite everything's that goin' on shawty." I kissed her hand as I held her close to me.

"Damn, I love the way you smell. You just do something to me." She stared into my eyes. "You always have."

"What the fuck are you doin' to me Sen?" I asked her seriously.

"Makin' you fall deeper and deeper in love with me each day." She pulled the tee shirt over her head.

I was gone all over again at the sight of her nakedness. As she positioned her body over mine, I shook my head.

"You doin' a damn good job," I took a deep breath knowing that after that time we needed to start using condoms.

It was going to be hard as hell, but there was no way I would be able to keep pulling out of that good ass pussy.

* * *

"JJ? What up my nigga?" I asked as I glanced at the time on my phone.

Shit, it was after two am. Sen was asleep on the sofa with her feet in my lap. I'd been nodding off watching TV. That shit was the life. A beautiful woman, chilling, no worries. Then I thought about it. The no worries part was a stretch.

"I need to come through for a minute," he said.

"Nah homey. It ain't a good time."

"What the fuck nigga? Although y'en tell me, I know you ain't wit' Lena no mo'. Dame told me 'bout that bitch and how yo' crazy ass nutted up on her nigga. Mufuckas think you on some chill, laid back shit, but yo' ass'll kill a nigga if need be," JJ spat like he was trying to suck up to me and shit.

He was right though. Niggas underestimated me, but that was how I wanted it to be.

"Why I gotta be wit' Lena for it not to be a good time? It's late nigga." I shook my head.

"I need some trees. I'm like two blocks from yo' crib man. C'mon. Hook a nigga up."

"Hook you up? So once again yo' broke ass tryna get a freebie?"

"Why you tryna play a nigga? You know I'm gon' get you back man."

I laughed. "Nigga, get me back? Fuck outta here. You ain't never paid me back for shit. You my nigga, but dayum. I'm just sayin' on some real nigga shit, you need to get it together man. For real."

"Get it together? What you sayin'?" He asked as if he was surprised.

"Nigga, you shocked? C'mon J. You gotta know this shit's gettin' tired and shit. You gotta stop gettin' over on your boys. How many times do I call you askin' for shit? Do I be dippin' in yo' closet to impress a bitch?"

"Oh, it's like that? You think you better than a nigga and shit 'cause you sell a lil' weed. Nigga, if it won't for yo' grandma's dough and your pop's connections you wouldn't be shit. You try to act all hard, but you soft as a fuckin' cotton ball. I said that bullshit earlier just to gas yo' head up nigga. Fuck you!"

"Oh, so that's how you feel nigga?"

"Suck on deez nuts mufucka!"

He hung up after saying that gay ass shit. All I could do was stare at the phone. Oh, hell nah. You could be cool with a nigga all your life before realizing that they'd been on some hating ass shit the whole time. So he had animosity because I was good and he was on some begging shit. Fuck nigga. He was on some bullshit, but it was alright. It just showed and proved that some niggas really did believe in keeping their enemies closer.

* * *

Sen had breakfast ready bright and early in the morning. Shawty had made waffles, turkey bacon, hash browns and scrambled eggs. I got full as hell before heading out early to handle my business.

"Thank you for everything Keys, but we gotta handle Trell soon. He keeps callin' makin' threats and shit."

I grabbed her hand and squeezed. "Don't worry. I'm meetin' wit' Dame today. At first I didn't wanna involve him, but now I think havin' the extra back up won't hurt since he proved himself after…"

She nodded. "Please don't bring that back up."

I moved her hair away from the bruise on her forehead. "How're you feelin'? Any weakness, dizziness…?"

"After I got into it with your ex hoe I felt a little dizzy, but I've been good since then." She continued to eat as I shook my head.

"You're something else yo'." I couldn't help but laugh.

"I'm just saying, she seems…I don't know, a little green."

"Green?"

"Yeah, you know what green means."

"Green is a color."

She shook her head. "Yeah and it's also a behavior. The bitch's naïve as hell. She ain't never been through a damn thing."

I nodded. "You might be right about that."

"I know that I'm right. She cried when I told her...about us." She chewed her food and then continued. "She's not over you and a woman scorned...well you know."

"That ain't nothing for you to worry about. Thanks for breakfast ma, but I gotta go handle some business. Like I said, don't answer the door for any fuckin' body. Don't be hard headed okay."

"I'm tired of bein' cramped inside." She pouted.

"Well, bein' cramped inside is best for you right now if you wanna stay alive." My voice was stern and she didn't talk back.

"Just have something for me soon baby. I just wanna get this over with." Her eyes were full of desperation.

"Ok shawty, I got you." We kissed again before I headed to the door.

When I left I couldn't help but worry about her. What if the people who were after her were already on to the fact that she was with me. If the price was right anybody could be found. I just hoped she'd follow my instructions and stay her ass inside. Until Trell and whoever was after her was eliminated she was in danger and she needed to act like it. In my eyes she didn't seem to be taking the threats to her life seriously enough.

* * *

My pop's phone kept going to the voicemail, but I had a key to the shed to get my shit myself. The thing was, I always felt better letting him know that I was on my way. True, he was my pops and the weed was mine as well, but it just felt like common courtesy. It was early, so I figured he was sleeping late.

About thirty minutes later I was pulling up in his driveway, but I noticed that his car wasn't there. Kelly's champagne colored Chrysler 300 was parked though. It was blocking my way to the back, so I grabbed the empty duffel bag that I had in the back seat. I guess I was going to have to just carry that shit back to my whip.

Before I could get out of the car Kelly was outside making her way toward me. Damn, I wasn't really in the mood to deal with her. All I wanted to do was grab my shit and be out.

"Keys! What's up?" She asked with that radiant smile on her face.

Why the hell did she have to be so damn attractive?

"Sup Kelly? Where my pops at?" I asked reminding her that she was with my father.

She was half naked as always and standing a little closer to me than she should've been.

"I'on know. He had a doctor's appointment earlier this mornin' and now he ain't been answerin' his phone," she said.

"Well, I'm just gon' get my shit and get up outta here. Tell him I came by and I tried to…"

To my surprise she pushed me against the car and grabbed my dick.

"You know I wanna fuck you right?" She licked her lips and then flashed a sexy look at me.

"Uh…" I grabbed her hand and pushed it away. "You my pop's girl yo'. What the fuck you think this is? I'on roll like that."

She sucked her teeth like she was offended. "Nigga, I see how you be lookin' at me. You want this pussy. Stop frontin' and shit." Her hand was on my dick again and I had to admit that I'd love to fuck the shit out of Kelly.

Instead I pushed her away again. The thing was, she was my pop's chick and I was falling in love with Sen. I wasn't trying to fuck up with the two most important people in my life. The pussy was probably hella good, but it wasn't worth losing my father and the woman that I loved.

"You fine as fuck Kelly. I won't deny that shit. To be real wit' you, if you wasn't wit' my pops I'd fuck the shit outta you, straight up ma. If you really care 'bout my old man though, you'll chill the fuck out and gone on in the house. I'll act like this shit never happened, 'cause I know it would fuck him up. He really cares about you yo'." Damn, I felt bad although I hadn't done shit.

There was a look of guilt on her face, but it faded quickly. "Yo' pops know what this is. He's a'ight and all, but since we bein' honest he can't fuck me right Keys. I mean, he can eat some pussy, but...'cause of the...you know...sometimes he just can't perform like that."

"Too much information yo'." I frowned my face up.

My pops had pulled out of the drug game because of two bullets that had hit him in the back five years ago. He was leaving a club when some random niggas decided that they were going to rob him and steal his whip. Since then he'd never been the same. The doctors originally said that he would be paralyzed from the waist down, but he defied the odds.

He could walk, but needed the aid of a cane sometimes. Often he would complain about numbness. I was aware of the fact that he sometimes took Viagra to stay hard. That really bothered him being that he had a thing for younger women. Even with the use of medication, he felt inadequate because he was too young to be suffering from Erectile Dysfunction. We both knew that it was due to what had happened to him, but obviously that hoe didn't understand.

I was pissed because my pops wanted to go right back to what had put him in the hospital fighting for his life back then, because of that ungrateful ass heifer standing in front of me.

"I won't tell him shit. We can keep it a secret. Damn." Her eyes were on mine. "I know you can fuck Keys. I can tell. You bow-legged and the way you walk is so fuckin' sexy."

"You gon' really keep tryin' ma? You that fuckin' thirsty to be dicked down? Damn. I ain't givin' you no dick. You want that shit too bad. I fuck good and I'on need you gettin' all obsessed wit' me and shit. I couldn't do that shit to my pops and I got a girl. Her pussy's the best I ever had, so I'm straight on that yo'."

Kelly propped her leg up on the hood of my car.

"What you doin'…" My voice trailed off when she lifted her skirt up and exposed her fat, waxed clean pussy.

I couldn't take my eyes off that shit because she had actually spread it open for me to get a good look at her swollen clit. When she pushed a finger inside of her pussy and pulled it out I saw the sheen of her juices. All I could do was shake my head. That shit was so tempting. The man in me wanted to bend her over and give it to her ass right outside.

"C'mon Keys…" She pulled her skirt up some more and revealed that shapely, round ass. "Just make me cum. I'm so serious when I say that you may think yo' girl's pussy is the best, but you ain't never had this. Why you think yo' dad's so fucked up over me? He's older and he done fucked plenty bitches. Her pussy might be good compared to what you had, but my shit is awesome nigga. When yo' pops shit will get hard I suck and fuck the shit outta him. I promise you ain't never had nothin' as tight and deep as this shit." As she pointed at her pretty ass pussy I snapped out of it and looked away.

Fuck, she was making it too hard for a nigga, but I wasn't going to do that shit. I had to focus on what I was there for and it wasn't to fuck her.

"Go head on yo'." I reluctantly walked toward the back of the house as she yelled behind me.

"Fuck you Keys! You could've fucked me in the ass and everything! I do it all!" That hoe had no shame as she continued. "I'll suck yo' balls and lick yo' asshole nigga! I'on give a fuck! I'm a nasty bitch!"

I just shook my head and stopped when I got to the shed. The locks had obviously been tampered with and the door was slightly opened.

"What the…?" I pulled the door open all the way. All of the work that I had stashed was gone.

My first thought was that bitch Kelly was trying to throw me off because she knew what the fuck was up. Then I thought it was strange that my pops was gone. The conversation I'd had with him about wanting to get back into the game raised red flags. I was ready to go off because I had at least 15 pounds left. That was a huge fucking investment and that shit was gone.

"What the fuck yo'!" I yelled and when I turned around that bitch Kelly was gone.

She couldn't have gone too far because her car was still there. My whip had her blocked in, so I figured that she was in the house. That shit was quick as hell though and I wondered if she'd ran off because she knew something. I quickly made my way back to the front of the house and rang the doorbell. After that I knocked on the door.

"What the fuck?" Kelly asked when I opened it. "You rejected me and now you at the door. What? You wanna take me up on my offer?"

I was ready to choke that bitch out. "Hell nah bitch! Do you know what the fuck happened to my shit?"

"Bitch?" She screwed her face up. "What the fuck? You a rude ass mufucka."

She genuinely seemed to not know what was going on, but I still wasn't convinced.

"My fuckin' weed is gone and I wanna know who the fuck took my shit!"

The look of fear on her face made me want to back down, but I was pissed. Instead of going off any further, I decided to just calm down and leave.

"Tell my pops to call me yo'," I spat through clenched teeth.

After that I turned and left because if I didn't I was going to murder that hoe. Something told me that she knew something and my pops did too.

Chapter 11

Jasenia

The sound of the door opening and then the beep of the alarm startled me as I watched a repeat of Love and Hip Hop Atlanta. I immediately sat up because of the loud sound of footsteps. My heart was pounding and I literally held my breath. Keys had made sure to get my gun from my condo and it was on the end table. Just as I was about to grab it Keys walked into the room.

"Hey babe," I said with a sigh of relief. "You're back already?"

There was a tight look on his face that made it clear to me that something was wrong.

"What happened?"

He shook his head and sat down beside me. "I went to get the work from my pop's crib and that shit was fuckin' gone yo'." I left out the part about that bitch coming on to me. I didn't want her to get upset.

Sen wasn't the type of woman to let some shit like that fly and I needed her ass to stay put.

She frowned at me. "What the fuck? Who took it?"

I shrugged my shoulders. "I'on know ma. Shit. I'm really hoping my pops wouldn't do no shady ass shit like that to me man. I'on trust that bitch he fuck wit' though." I filled her in on my pops telling me that he wanted to get back in the game and the fact that Kelly was the reason behind it.

Sen shook her head. "She sounds like my mother. Money hungry ass hoe. What are you going to do?"

"I'm gon' wait 'till my pops gets home and then I'm gonna go and talk to him. Straight up, man to man. After that I'on know ma. Damn!" He sighed and pulled his phone from his pocket.

I just sat there in silence as he made a call. The stress on his face showed, but despite that, he was still sexy as fuck.

"Dame, sup man?" There was a short pause and then he continued. "I'm 'bout to come through and holla at you."

My thoughts drifted and I wanted to go with him to talk to Dame about what to do about Trell. The danger of me leaving his spot was real, but I felt the need to be involved in the planning. I mean, it was my life and my father's that was at stake.

When Keys ended the call he interrupted my musing.

"Babe, I'm 'bout to head out for a minute. I just needed to see yo' pretty face first." He leaned over and kissed me.

"So, you're going to talk to Dame about the situation with Trell right?" My voice was eager as I asked.

"Yeah, I gotta let him know that I ain't got the work too. He gon' have to wait for me to reup again, but I'll handle that later. I gotta hit up yo' pops and shit."

I wrung my hands together. "I…uh…I want to go with you to talk to Dame."

That nigga looked at me like I had lost every ounce of sense I was born with.

"What?" I asked. "I mean, I think I should be there. This is my life we're talkin' about here. It's not like…"

He shook his head defiantly. "No, you're stayin' here ma. Whatever we talk about I'll discuss wit' you when I get back."

Tears stung my eyes. I was going stir crazy, because I wasn't used to sitting still that long. Being stuck inside was making me feel like a prisoner.

"I feel like I'm in prison Keys."

"I think your so called prison is better than a grave right now ma. I'on know 'bout you."

I sighed because he was right.

"Okay," I huffed.

"Look Sen. I'm gonna keep it one hundred wit' you. You gotta start makin' smarter decisions about shit. You're too damn intelligent to keep gettin' yourself into reckless shit. For every action there's a fuckin' reaction and you know that. After we handle shit wit' Trell and the mufuckas who tryna kill you, you gon' have to work on that. A'ight? I love you and I ain't tryna lose you."

My eyes were casted down because his honesty was raw. I felt his hand on my face and then he lifted my chin to make me look at him.

"You're absolutely right. It's time for me to grow the fuck up," I agreed.

He kissed me again.

"I'll be back in a few hours, so stay yo' ass here. You got everything you need. If something happens call me. A'ight."

I nodded and walked him to the door. Before he could leave I wrapped my arms around his neck and held him tight. As I did I inhaled the scent of his cologne. It was intoxicating.

"Be careful."

His lips were on my ear. "I will." Then they were on my neck setting my body on fire again. Damn.

With reluctance he finally pulled away from me and left. I quickly locked the door and flopped back down on the sofa. My phone was vibrating on the coffee table and I didn't really feel like talking to anybody. Hopefully it wasn't Nadia because I didn't feel like trying to hide shit from her. After picking the phone up, I saw that it was Trell.

"Yeah," I answered in annoyance.

"Sen, baby…"

Suddenly I felt brave as I cut him off. "Don't baby me Trell. We both know the point of this so called relationship, so let's stop pretending. I'm not going to try to convince my father that we're in love even if he finds out about us. Honestly, I just want you to keep your end of the bargain. You already got me stuck between a rock and a hard place, so why keep on pushing. I'll help you get what the fuck you want, but I just want you to leave me alone otherwise. Once you get what you want, I want the video. That's it. You can go your way and I'll go mine. This fake ass couple bullshit is for the birds. I'm done acting for your benefit." There, it was out. I just hoped that he was buying it.

The line was quiet and I thought he'd hung up on me. "Trell?"

He cleared his throat. "You must be losin' yo' mind bitch. We a fuckin' couple 'till I say we ain't."

I let out a deep sigh of frustration and tears came to my eyes. I willed them away. It was not the time to show him a sign of weakness. He wouldn't even hear my voice crack.

"You wanna kill me don't you?" He suddenly asked.

His taunting was really making me want to put a bullet in his skull, but I kept it cool. "I just want you to leave me the fuck alone Trell."

"Well I ain't gon' leave you alone bitch. Not 'till I'm fuckin' ready. You do what the fuck I say. I got the upper fuckin' hand. Too bad you can't kill me. I already told my niggas that if I end up dead you did that shit. They already know to go ahead and send the video to the fuckin' cops. After that they gon' murk you, yo' best friend and yo' hoe ass mama. Then after yo' pops get locked up for murder he gon' get murked. You wouldn't be able to kill me if you wanted to. I'll put a bullet in yo' fine ass so fast and then fuck you while you dyin' bitch." His wicked laughter sent chills all over my body. "That's how good that pussy is. I'll finally get to hit that shit raw."

If only he knew that Keys was getting this good pussy and he'd never get to even smell it again. How could he threaten to kill me and fuck my dead body? That nigga was probably the coldest motherfucker I knew. Not only did he want to rob my father, but he wanted to continue to fuck me. Like I could really keep sleeping with the enemy. I wasn't built like that. My temper came from my father and mother, so my temptation to go ahead and end his life was strong as hell. My conscience kept telling me to take a taxi close to his place and just get it over with. Then the thought of him doing exactly what he'd threatened to do crossed my mind.

"You just gotta make this shit hard I see. What the fuck is up with you and your damn control issues? I'm wondering if you need some medication or something you asshole."

He let out a snide cackle. "Fuck what you talkin' 'bout woman. Maybe I do need some medication and shit. Right now money and pussy is all the medicine I need bitch. Know that. If yo' ass don't be back in Atlanta by tomorrow I'm makin' a trip to Miami to drag yo' ass back. You fuckin' hear me?"

The laughter was gone.

"I hear you. Can I go now nigga?"

"I see that you smellin' yourself. We gon' fix that when you get back. Later."

I hung up and rolled my eyes. It was going to take some convincing for Keys to let me go around Trell. If I didn't show him that I was in Atlanta the next day I had no clue if he'd go to Miami to hurt Nadia. It was fucked up because at first I thought him going to Miami would give me a break, but it didn't occur to me that he'd be a threat to her. He had met her before and I was sure that if he wanted to he could find her.

My fucked up choices had put everybody that I cared about in danger, even Keys. My soul yelled for me to just call my daddy and tell him the truth about everything. He'd be mad as hell, but I knew that his love for me surpassed any judgment. Yet and still, I couldn't taint myself in his eyes. I just couldn't.

* * *

"Girl, you better be careful," Nadia advised me about my relationships with Keys and Trell.

I called her because after not wanting to talk, I needed to hear her voice. My best friend meant the world to me. Growing up I had more male friends than female friends. Nadia was really the only chick I'd clicked with. She was cool as fuck, but she'd pop off in a second.

One thing about me was, I didn't fuck with weak bitches. If you were my ace you had to be ready for whatever. When we were in a club or somewhere and some hating ass bitches got out of pocket I needed a ride or die with me. That was exactly what Nadia was, but even with her brave nature and sassiness, I knew that she was no match for Trell. I just wanted my girl to be safe.

"I am. I have a plan girl. No worries. I'm working on getting rid of Trell." She just didn't know that I meant that shit in a permanent way.

"Hmm, okay boo. When you comin' down to see me, or maybe I should come there. Shit, I should come this weekend..."

I killed that thought real damn quick. "I'll come down there soon boo. Last time you came down here you know what happened. These ATL niggas are a different breed." The laugh I managed to let out sounded artificial and I hoped my bestie couldn't read me.

"What's really goin' on Sen? You don't sound right. You know I'on give a fuck about no niggas. I got my man."

Damn her, I thought.

She knew me all too well, but I had to play it off.

"I'm good. Ain't nothing going on girl. Well, nothing other than me loving Keys. That nigga unlocked my heart for real. He got me so gone Nadia. He is literally giving me life." I thought about that last statement. It was true. That nigga was hell bent on keeping me alive.

"You always talked about him bitch. I should've known. How did a childhood friendship turn into love so fast?" She sounded skeptical, but I knew that it was real.

"Because it was meant to be. The stars were aligned for me and Keys to be together. It's like...gravity... It's gonna happen whether we like or not.

I'm drawn to him like a magnet Di. It's like…it's like…"
I couldn't find the words. "When we make love it's like
we've been together before in another life. Like we're
going to keep getting reincarnated and reunited. It sounds
crazy, but it's really no other way to explain it. It's
fate…destiny. I couldn't fight that shit even if I tried."

"Wow bitch, that was deep as hell. What the fuck
you smokin' on? I need some of that shit!" She laughed,
but all I could do was smile.

Tears burned my eyes as I painted a pretty picture
for my friend, but I held them back. Shit, at that point I
was tired of crying. I needed her not to worry about me.
The stress wasn't good for her since she had just found
out that she was three months pregnant. I was happy for
her and her boyfriend of two years. His name was Jason
and he was a sweet heart. They'd gone through a
temporary break up during our little tryst with those
niggas in Atlanta. I was happy for my friend and if
anything happened to her I'd fuck a nigga up.

"No you don't. My niece or nephew don't need to
be getting high with your ass."

She laughed louder that time. "Boo, you just don't
know. I can't wait until I push this lil' mufucka out so I
can get fucked up."

My best friend meant the world to me and her
safety as well as the safety of her child was my concern.
Trell had to be handled asap and I couldn't wait for Keys
to come back with something. I really needed to be able
to move on to the next thing, which was eliminating the
other threat to my life. How we were going to do that, I

didn't know. That was a whole different level of strategizing. To be honest I had no idea who was really after me.

"Your ass is crazy. I'll call you back boo. Keys is calling me." I lied to get off the phone, but I wished he really was calling.

"K boo, love ya!"

"J'adore tu. Au'revoir."

"Whatever bitch. You know I don't speak no damn French," she laughed.

"Later chica."

I ended the call and sat there staring off into space. What if it was my time? What if it was easier to succumb to death? Shit, that thought was crazy. Life was just beginning for me. I'd just found the love of my life and there was so much that we had to experience. Like Keys had said, we could be a power couple. I could complete my degree and he could go legit. We'd be like Barack and Michelle Obama. I was a smart, classy fashionista like her and he was handsome and charismatic like him. Nah, death was not an option. I was going to fight to live. The crazy thing was, I hadn't always thought that way. Thank God for Keys. I knew that a man shouldn't validate my happiness, but with him in my life for such a short time, I felt so whole.

* * *

Boredom finally took over me and I fell asleep on the sofa. Of course sleep didn't come easy, but when it did I welcomed it. I figured I'd need the energy to handle what I was going through with Trell and a faceless killer that I didn't even know. Not having a clue of who would be coming after me was some stressful shit.

Being that it was hard to sleep the sound of the alarm beeping made me wake up. When I looked up Keys was standing there.

"Mind if I turn on the light?" He asked.

"Nah, go ahead." I sat up and gave him my undivided attention. "Please tell me something good."

He leaned over and turned the lamp on before sitting down. After giving me a soft peck on the lips he took a deep breath. His eyes were on mine and I could tell that what was going on was finally taking a toll on him. Damn, I felt horrible. Maybe it was best for me to leave him alone and deal with my bullshit myself.

"We gon' run up on that nigga Friday night."

That was in two days.

"We know he'll normally be leavin' the pool hall on Gresham Rd. that he always go to round two am. It's easier to catch him out instead of runnin' up in his crib. He might change his plans, so we gon' have to do something to keep tabs on that nigga. The thing is, I don't want you involved. I want you to stay far away from Trell…"

"I have to see him before that happens Keys. If I don't he's going to know that something is up. Not only that, but maybe I can find out who else has access to the video."

He shook his head. "Hell nah yo'. You won't be seein'…"

"He needs to think I'm not gonna change my mind and stay in Miami. That nigga threatened to kill my best friend. I can't chance that. If I don't see him he's gonna go to Miami because he thinks I'm there. I know he'll find her if he wants."

Keys sighed deeply. I could see the torment on his face. "If he touches you I'm gonna murk that nigga myself. Then that's gonna blow everything, because we don't really know if that video of what Mendosa did will make it to the police anyway. The only point of me not blastin' him right now is 'cause we gotta get that shit."

"Right. I can't chance my pops gettin' locked up or killed because of me. It's a possibility that nobody else knows and Trell's just using that to rattle me. Still, I don't want to take that chance." I didn't even mention the fact that Trell threatened to kill my mom. Honestly, I'd lost all respect for her and really didn't give a shit if she lived or not.

It was just that I didn't have the heart to put that bitch out of her misery myself. She had given me life whether she was a good mother or not. There was no way I could kill her. Still, I wouldn't give a damn if somebody else did.

"We could do that shit sooner, but the two of us haven't been on a date yet. For some reason I need us to do some normal shit before… I actually wanna take you out tomorrow. It won't be anywhere around here though. We gon' go to Charleston, SC and stay overnight. Is that cool?" He asked and then kissed my cheek.

"Yes, I'd love that."

"Once we get Trell outta the way we gon' have to find out who's after you ma. They might not send somebody else right away, but I'm sure they will eventually. I can't chance that shit." He pulled me close to him and held me tight.

"I'm scared Keys…"

"I know." His voice was a whisper. "If you feel that it's a must for you to see Trell I'll let you, but under one condition."

"What?" I was almost afraid to know.

"I'm gonna be there."

"What? No Keys. He'll kill you and we don't want him to know about us. He's crazy Keys."

"He won't know. I'm just gonna follow you and park not far from where ya'll will be. I want you to call me and put the phone on speaker. Just make sure you keep the phone where I can hear what's goin' on. After you let him see that you're still here and workin' on findin' out where yo' pop's reserve is make up a reason to leave and shit. That's the only way I'm lettin' you see that nigga. You right, he's crazy, but he ain't as crazy as I am about you. I ain't lettin' shit happen to you Sen. Fuck that."

When I turned to look at him I could see the passion that he felt for me etched on his tired face. I nodded in agreement.

"Okay, that'll work baby, but you look tired. Let's go to sleep."

A sly smile made his eyes light up. "We ain't 'bout to be sleepin' ma."

I laughed. "No, we're going to sleep tonight. We have tomorrow for everything else."

He smiled as he stretched. "You're right ma. I am tired as hell."

"So, did you talk to your father about what happened?"

He nodded. "He claims he don't know what the fuck happened and Kelly too. I'on know shawty. I'll handle that later though. We got more pressin' shit goin' on. I went to see your pops today to reup and handled that transaction for Dame. That shit actually didn't go left like I thought it would. Still, I suffered a loss wit' 15 bricks gone."

"C'mon baby." After grabbing his hand I led him to the bedroom and undressed him. Once he was down to his boxers we climbed under the covers. Without saying a word about anything we just held each other close knowing that we couldn't predict what was going to happen. All I knew was I was feeling the shit out of Keys and I wished I could turn back the hands of time and change things. Being happy with him was all that I wanted, but our future seemed so uncertain.

Chapter 12

Keys

"Pops, man, who else could've done it then? It's mighty funny that my shit's gone right after you told me you wanted to get back in the game. If you needed some money you could've just asked." My eyes were glued to his face because I wanted to see his reaction.

The night before we had only talked on the phone, but I thought it was important for us to talk face to face. I'd be going with Sen to throw Trell off and then we'd be on our way to South Carolina. After that it would be on to getting rid of that fuck nigga. I had no idea how things would turn out, so I felt the need to confront my pops before it all went down.

"I didn't take that shit Keys." His eyes were sincere.

"Well Kelly did then."

He shook his head in disagreement. "She wouldn't do that."

"Which takes me back to the question of who the fuck did it then."

He sighed and gathered his thoughts. I could tell because that's how he was. My pops used to be an angry, disrespectful ass dude, but he changed after he got shot. Nowadays he'd think about things before he said them, so I waited.

"I don't know who did it Keys. I wish I did. When I got up I should've checked, but nothing like that has happened before. I went to my doctor's appointment and Kelly was at her mother's for a while. She got back here a few minutes before you did and I'm sure she didn't know that the shed had been broken into."

All I could do was shake my head. "Why the fuck do you trust that money hungry bitch? She ain't right for you, but you can't see past that hoe's pussy. What the hell makes you think she won't rob me? Huh? She ain't loyal to you, so why would I expect that hoe to be loyal to me."

"What you sayin' son?" His eyes were hard and I could tell that he was pissed. "You ain't gotta call her bitches and hoes. Why you gotta disrespect her like that?"

"I ain't gon' sugar coat shit for you pops. You already know that bitch ain't shit." I'd already said too much, so I decided to shut my mouth about that hoe.

"Ain't nobody perfect Keys. Shit, you ain't got no proof she did shit…"

I stood up and cut him off. "And you ain't got proof that she didn't. I'm out pops. I see that I ain't gon' find out what happened like this."

My father pleaded with me. "Son, I swear, I would never do you like that and Kelly won't either. Somebody else did it. Think about who knows that you leave your shit here. Who have you told?"

"I'll holla at you," I said as I walked out of the house.

When I got in my car I thought about what he had said. Something told me that Kelly had something to do with that shit and was trying to throw me off by offering me the pussy. Then I thought about who actually did know that I kept my work there. Who had I told? I was a private nigga and I didn't let others in on my business. Then suddenly a light bulb went off in my head. Hmmm…

* * *

About two hours later I was sitting in my car listening to Trell and Jasenia's conversation. At that point it sounded pretty civil for him.

"Look, you see that I'm here now. I have to go," she said suddenly.

She'd already explained that she was still working on getting the information that she needed to get him off her back.

"Go the fuck where?" He asked angrily. "I didn't tell you you could leave bitch?"

That got my attention. I knew that he was going to start snapping. That mufucka was going to make me go inside and get that shit over and done with. That was all I wanted anyway, but Sen was worried about what he had on her father. She didn't want her actions and decisions to destroy anybody else. That was some stand up shit, but what had to be done had to be done.

My hand was on my tool and I was ready to go in that bitch.

"If you keep talking to me like that you'll never get what you want. Eventually I'm going to get tired of that shit and say fuck it. I've never been interested in my father's lifestyle before now Trell. It's going to take time for me to find out where his reserve is without him being suspicious. Let me do this the right way so we can both walk away from this shit."

There was nothing but silence for a moment. "Yeah, whatever. Just take yo' ass to Mendosa and get to diggin'. A'ight."

"Okay, damn. I just wish you had kept this between us. Your boys didn't have to know about what my dad did. I know that he took someone that you love away from you, but that has nothing to do with me. Why the fuck are you punishing me?"

"Because you're part of him bitch. All those years of not knowin' what happened to my pops changed everything for me. I was determined to find out what happened to him. Before I even knew that Mendosa killed him I wanted you. Now I got both of the things I wanted the most. I guess it's the way I got 'em that's fucked up. After I get what I want from yo' pops I still want you. You ain't goin' nowhere bitch. I mean that shit. You stuck wit' me. If you ever leave me I'm gon' make sure you pay for that shit."

Suddenly the call was disconnected and I knew that it was a possibility that her life was in danger. I was getting out of the car with my gun in my hand when I saw Sen walking out of the house. She was wiping her eyes and I could tell that she was feeling defeated about everything. I wanted to go over to her and hold her in my arms, but I couldn't. When she got in her car and drove off I waited a few minutes to pull off behind her.

* * *

Sen broke down in my arms time we got back to my place. She didn't want to talk about what had happened over the phone. Only two minutes had gone by during the time that I couldn't hear what she and Trell were saying. I wanted to know what that nigga had said.

"What the fuck he say?" I asked with an attitude. Shit, the desire to kill that nigga was too damn strong and if she said the word I was going to do it.

"His boy JJ got a copy of the video…"

"JJ?" I asked automatically thinking about that fuck nigga. With his begging ass. It wouldn't surprise me if he was hanging on to Trell's coattails, but that would be the ultimate betrayal. According to him, he didn't fuck with Trell like that.

"Yup, he said JJ," she confirmed.

I sighed without elaborating about why I needed her confirmation. I'd just have to find out later if that nigga JJ really fucked with Trell. Maybe he'd said another name. Me and that nigga JJ had had a misunderstanding, but we'd had them before. It wouldn't surprise me if he was disloyal, but damn. "Did you put the bug somewhere?"

She nodded. "Yes, I managed to put it under the coffee table in the living room when he wasn't looking."

The listening device was our way of finding out where the original video was, who else had a copy and where he'd be the night we planned to do the hit. Hopefully he'd talk about that shit within the next twenty four hours. In the meantime I was going to try to push the bullshit out of my mind and enjoy my woman. Thoughts of Elena, Trell, JJ and whoever was after my girl were on the back burner...for now.

"You got yo' shit packed right?"

She nodded. "Yeah, but are you sure we should..."

"Hell yeah. I'on know 'bout you ma, but I need this. If I don't get away I'm gon' kill that son of a bitch tonight."

She wrapped her arms around me as I wiped the tears from her eyes.

* * *

We left the house with her in somewhat of a disguise. She'd taken her sew in out and her natural hair texture was curly spirals that stopped at her shoulder blades. I loved her hair like that. There was no makeup on her face and she had on a pair of dark, oversized shades. It was funny how I wanted her more than ever at that moment.

It took a little over four hours to get to Charleston because we only made one stop for gas. Gas was so much cheaper in South Carolina, so I was sure to fill up. The next stop was the beautiful log cabin that my father owned. It was in the booneys, but it was safe. There were no neighbors for miles, so we didn't have to worry about

Sen being found by her enemies or some crazy redneck attacking us.

"Wow, I'm impressed Keys. This place is...so beautiful. I can imagine how it would look if it snowed. I've never been a country girl, but I needed this baby. Thank you," she said once we were inside.

I held her close to me and inhaled the scent of her shampoo as we walked around the place. It was two stories with three bedrooms, three and a half baths, a breakfast nook, huge modern kitchen with stainless steel appliances, dining room, den, living room and a finished basement.

"I would've got us a nice suite by the water, but I didn't want to chance it."

My eyes were on her with a smile as she ventured off to the door that led to the back yard. The view was amazing because there was a lake that was only a few feet away from the patio.

"Oh my God. This is amazing Keys. Simple, but amazing." She sounded breathless as she spoke. "Ducks and everything. We could go ice skating in the winter. I'm in love with this place."

I walked up behind her and wrapped my arms around her waist. Her soft hands gently caressed mine.

"Well, I figured that you've seen pretty much everything, so why not just show you something so natural and like you said, simple."

"Yeah, because when I came here before we stayed in a suite at a resort. Once we got a log cabin in Aspen on a skiing trip, but that was nothing like this."

I hated to leave her, but it wasn't shit in the house. I had to make a trip to the store, which would take a while. "I need to go get some things. After that we'll go out to eat. I want to take you on a real date, but I didn't want to do it in Atlanta. I think we could sneak out for a little bit and go somewhere. I know the perfect place. It's a seafood restaurant on the pier. Most times it's pretty busy, so we can just blend in. Would you like that?"

I kissed her shoulder as she nodded. "Yes. I love seafood."

"Okay. I won't be gone long baby. There's not even any water in the fridge. I don't want you wanting for shit."

She turned to face me and then planted a sweet kiss on my lips. "I'll be fine baby. Nobody knows we're here. Relax. I'll be waiting for you when you get back."

I left her reluctantly and climbed behind the wheel of the car. There was an alarm system in the house and I set it before leaving. It was a little bit after six pm and the restaurant didn't close until one am. I had plenty of time for us to get dressed after we messed around a little bit.

* * *

On the way back from the grocery store I made a call to Dame. He was the one who had got the bug for me to put in Trell's spot. That nigga had all types of connections and could get his hands on anything. He fucked with this Federal Agent named Sammy, or some code shit. That nigga got the bug and set it up so that

Dame could listen to what was going on from his computer. I was amazed at how easy it was.

Before Sen planted it we made sure that it was on. It had been tested by us talking even a few feet away from the device. Dame could hear us loud and clear, so I knew that it would work. Once we'd left Trell's Dame called to confirm that he could hear everything.

"Sup nigga. I know what you callin' for, but that nigga ain't said shit we can use yet."

"You talked to that nigga JJ?"

"Nah, that mufucka's avoidin' me, but we got a plan for that. When you get back tomorrow we gon' go see his ass. You know play it cool and shit. Then we gon' find that damn video and pop his ass."

I nodded like he could see me. "A'ight nigga. Holla at me if you get something."

"Will do my nigga."

I hung up and gunned it so that I could get back to Sen. We had just talked and she said that she was about to run a bubble bath. Shit, I told her she better wait for me. A nigga was ready to see all of that fineness all nice and wet.

* * *

Sen was just lowering her body into the water when I walked in the bathroom. She didn't even bother to pin her hair up. I figured if it got wet, she'd just let it air dry, which was fine with me. Like I said before, I liked her natural state. Her glamorous look had lured me in, but I think I liked her better minus the weave, expensive clothes and make up. When we met we were just kids, so I loved her no matter what.

"There was some bubble bath, so I figured why not." She shrugged her shoulders.

"And I told you to wait for me."

She let out a laugh. "I did. You see that I just got in."

I quickly stripped out of my clothes and got in with her.

"I didn't even put the stuff I got in the fridge." My pops and Kelly must've visited recently because there was soap and bubble bath in the bathroom.

"It's okay baby. We won't be in here long. It won't spoil."

I smiled not wanting anything about what was going on in Atlanta to come up. It was a good thing that it didn't.

"This is the life ma." My voice was low and deep, which was meant to entice her.

She leaned back into my chest. "Yes it is."

I just wished it could always be that peaceful and serene. That part, I kept to myself. Like I said before, I didn't want to spoil the moment.

"So, out of all the places you've been, which is your favorite?" I kissed her shoulder and felt her body shiver.

"Anywhere you are."

I was taken aback. She'd been to so many places, but her favorite place was anywhere with me. That shit really made me feel some type of way.

"Damn ma," I shook my head. "I don't know what to say."

"Don't say anything." She turned around in the water to face me.

The tub was a large, round garden tub, so it was easy for her to maneuver her body. Her legs were on the side of mine and she was sitting on my lap.

I let out a groan in appreciation of the deep, sweet kiss we shared. "Mmm, Sen, look, we can't keep fuckin' without a condom. Not unless you wanna get pregnant."

"I'm on the pill," she simply said as she kissed my neck.

Damn, I was ready to get up in that shit.

"Well, what if the pill doesn't work."

She shrugged her shoulders and kissed me again. After that she lowered her wet, warmness down on my dick until I was all the way inside. Damn, I was in there nice and deep.

"Mmm, Keys..." she stared at me and I stared back in complete awe.

The sound of the water splashing as she grinded and thrust all over my shit mixed in tune with the melody of our moans and groans.

"Fuck...Sen...shiiiiit...." My eyes were glued to hers as we both came and clung to each for dear life.

Her lips were on my neck as we both caught our breath.

"Keys, I swear, your dick is too damn good. I see myself being so crazy over you."

"Hmm, you just don't know the half." I held on to her and thought about how fucked up I was over her ass already.

There was nothing in the world that could split us apart. Not even death, because our souls would forever be connected.

* * *

It was after ten when we got to Fleet Landing Restaurant. Sen was looking all good in a short, beige, t shirt dress with high splits on the sides that showed off her shapely hips and legs. The sandals that she wore were brown and flat, which was different for her. I was used to seeing her in heels. She seemed so carefree and comfortable as we walked inside of the restaurant holding hands. My hope was to see her like that more often.

Once we were seated by the water I ordered a Corona with lime and she ordered some kind of sweet cocktail. The sound of Sea Gulls flying overhead created the perfect ambience.

"It's a nice night." Sen observed. "The breeze coming off the water is perfect."

"You're perfect."

She blushed. "Shit, not by a long shot."

"You're perfect for me."

We ordered our food, sipped our drinks and talked. The night was indeed perfect and I wished we could have more moments like that. After everything was taken care of and shit fell into place we could finally have a real relationship. For the time being we'd steal those moments when we could. Watching her lips move as she talked, I appreciated the little things more than ever.

"Did you hear me babe?" Her voice broke me out of my trance.

"Uh, I'm sorry…I was caught up in your beauty."

"Stop playing." She laughed and I couldn't help but stare. "I said do you want children one day."

That made my heart drop because according to Elena I might've been having a child sooner than I'd planned.

"Yeah, one day, but not right now."

"Me too, but I don't want to ruin my figure. Isn't that selfish?"

I laughed. "That won't matter to you after we're married and stuff. Naturally you're going to want kids."

She grinned at me and then kissed my cheek. "Aww, after we're married and stuff. You're so fuckin' cute. Well, I kind of wanted to be a dancer before the smart side of me decided to take over. I took ballet, jazz, tap, contemporary and hip hop dance classes. My first two years of college I danced in the band and in high school I was in a dance troupe. At first I was really good at it, but I haven't really danced in a while. Well, not like that."

"That explains that bangin' ass body and how you can put your legs behind your head and shit. Mmm, that shit's so fuckin' sexy."

"Hmm, you haven't seen all of my tricks yet. My pops built a dance studio in the basement of the house in McDonough. When...everything's good...we'll go there and I'll dance for you."

"Shit, you can dance for me tonight."

We both laughed. "Okay...your wish is my command...my King."

I kissed her hand, her lips, her nose, her eyes and then her forehead. "I wanna kiss something else...my Queen," I whispered lustfully.

She looked around and then her wide eyes were back on me. "What? Not here Keys." Her ass was smiling and I could tell that the forbidden act excited her.

"Nobody's even sittin' close to us. It's late so the crowd's wearin' down. It's a long ass table cloth on the table and shit. Won't nobody even know what's goin' on. Only you." I winked at her. "Why you think I told you not to wear no panties? You my appetizer ma."

The look on her face said it all, but she was still being defiant. "What if the server comes...?"

"Let me serve you and make you cum." Shit, a nigga was as serious as a heart attack and a stroke at the same time. "That mufucka'll think I'm in the restroom. Unless you give that shit away wit' those sexy faces and the moans I know you gon' wanna let out."

"Why are you making this so hard?" Her facial expression told me that she wanted it.

"Do I ask you that when you make me hard? Don't question yo' man ma. I'on like that shit."

"Bossy…I like that. Fuck it." She looked around again. "Okay."

Swiftly, I was under that table tracing her smooth, thick ass thigh with kisses. She instinctively opened her legs for me to get up in there like I wanted.

"Mmmm," I moaned as the sweet flavor of her essence greeted my tongue.

She tasted so good. I could tell that she was into it because her hand was on my head and she was grinding and shit. Then a few minutes later she stopped moving and I heard her say, "Uhh…thank you…" My baby's voice was all shaky and low.

A nigga still didn't stop though. I guess our food had arrived, but my mouth was already full.

* * *

On the way back to Atlanta the next day a feeling of dread took over me. I wasn't scared of facing that nigga Trell, but I didn't know what was going to happen. We still didn't know when Will's people were going to strike again. I was sure that they knew that Sen was still alive at that point. Not hearing anything from a hit man to confirm the hit would let whoever hired him know that.

"You good baby?" Sen asked as she rubbed the back of my neck. That shit was so relaxing to me.

I didn't say yes or no. "I will be once you're safe."

She sighed. "Every time reality sets in I hate myself Keys. I shouldn't have ever drug you into this. I…"

"Stop, please. Sometimes in life there's shit you just can't control. The way I feel for you is one of them. I'm all in now baby, so it's no gettin' rid of me."

"But what if something happens to you?" Her voice was full of panic. "What will I do then?"

I glanced over at her. "Look Sen, when it comes to the streets I may not be on the same scale as Mendosa, but I ain't no scared ass nigga. As you know I will shoot my gun, but I don't do dumb shit. I'm goin' handle everything ma. Once Trell is out the way we gon' do what we gotta do to keep you alive. Even if we gotta leave and go somewhere. Maybe you can get that person you know to doc me up a passport and shit."

"Damn, I'm a lucky ass woman Keys." She shook her head. "I never looked at it that way, until now."

My phone rang just as I rubbed her thigh. I didn't want to, but I pulled my hand away to answer it since I was driving. It was Dame.

"Sup man? Please tell me you got something?"

"Hell yeah. That nigga Trell can't keep his mouth shut. Yo' girl was right man. JJ is fuckin' wit' that nigga. He was at that nigga's crib earlier. I recognized his voice. That shit burnt me up, but you know I fucks with Mendosa, so I ain't do no dumb shit like run up in there sprayin'. We gotta make sure we get that evidence first."

Then my mind drifted to something else. "Word, well you know I told you 'bout my shit gettin' taken right? I mean, I ain't tryna say you did shit, but I ain't tell nobody but you man."

"Wow, for real nigga?" Dame laughed. "I'on even fuck wit' that shit like that. Why the hell would I do it? I mean, c'mon man, I always been down for you. Loyal is my middle fuckin' name man."

"You right nigga. You ain't never did no crooked ass shit to me, but I'on even know about loyalty these days."

"Y'en gotta question mine man. We on the same team. Straight the fuck up."

"A'ight my nigga. I'll be at the crib in 'bout two hours. I'll hit you up."

"A'ight."

* * *

Time I pulled up in the driveway that nigga Dame called me and dropped another bomb.

"We ain't gon' be able to get that nigga Trell tonight," he said.

"Why the fuck not?" I asked feeling agitated. My patience was running thin as hell. "I thought he was plannin' to go to the pool hall on Gresham. What happened to followin' his ass from there?"

"I just heard that nigga on the phone wit' somebody talkin' 'bout his moms is dyin' and shit. She sick, but he ain't say what's wrong. He left to go to Savannah where she at. Turns out that bitch is in a mental hospital and shit. She schizo or some shit."

"Yeah, I heard about that."

"That nigga's on his way to see her and he ain't say how long he gon' be there."

"Fuck!" I was pissed off.

"What?" Sen asked. Her eyes were on me.

"A'ight man. We gotta regroup and shit. For now we gon' just concentrate on that nigga JJ. At least we can find the video and see what he knows."

The thought of not getting Trell when we planned made me even more enraged than before. I was ready to put a bullet in his head and destroy the damn evidence he had on Mendosa, but that mufucka was on his way out of town.

When I ended the call with Dame I filled Sen in on what was going on. The tears were visible in her eyes and then her phone rang. She looked up at me.

"It's Trell."

Chapter 13

Jasenia

"Hello," I answered the call wishing he'd just leave me the fuck alone and go see his mother.

The freedom of knowing that he was going to be away for a while was inviting.

"Look bitch, I'm on the way to handle some business and I'on know when I'll be back to the A. That gives you time to find out where yo' pops shit at. Until then I'll have somebody watchin' you. If you make a move that I'on like all the threats I made gon' happen. You hear me bitch."

I had put the phone on speaker and Keys looked like he was going to explode at any second.

"Okay." I decided to comply just so he'd go ahead and take his ass to Savannah.

"I'll be in touch. Keep my pussy tight or I'm gon' choke you out like that nigga did my pops. Don't get slick 'cause like I told you, if you try something my nigga got word to do what I was gonna do wit' that video. A'ight bitch. Later."

He hung up and we both just sat there in the car for a minute. I shook my head.

"I wish I had known this shit was going to happen. I would've steered clear of that fuckin' nut job. He is a waste of sperm and I can't wait until his ass is dead."

When I felt his arms around me I felt better instantly. "I just wanted to get it over with. It's too damn much Keys. I don't know how much I can handle before I…before I…"

Shit. I had to shut my mouth. If I said too much he'd run for the hills. He couldn't know about my past. The present was bad enough.

"Before you what baby?" His voice was full of concern, but I played it off.

"Nothing. I'm fine." I took a breath to calm myself down. "I just had a moment baby. It's nothing okay. Drop it."

His eyes were on me, penetrating my soul. He was looking for answers that I just wasn't ready to give him.

"Is that scar on your wrist nothing?"

I had to look away. "Not right now Keys." Before he could say anything else I got out of the car.

He followed me, but didn't say anything as he unlocked the door.

"Ladies first," he said as he gestured with his hand for me to walk inside.

Once the door was closed and we were sitting on the sofa he asked, "Why won't you just tell me what's really up wit' you Sen?"

"This isn't the time Keys, okay. I'm not ready. When I'm ready I'll tell you everything. You want too much too soon and I can't give you that. You have to be patient with me. Please. I've already told you enough."

He sighed and then stood up. "I gotta go. Stay here." That was all he said before he headed to the door. There was no hug or kiss like usual.

"You mad at me?" I asked knowing that he was at least a little pissed off. Shit was already getting to him and my elusive attitude wasn't helping.

"Nah ma. I'm just tryna understand you. That's all. I gotta go and check Dame out so we can at least see what's up wit' that nigga JJ. I'll call you when I can."

He opened the door and left without looking back. After the beautiful night and morning we'd had in South Carolina, I was disappointed about how distant we seemed now.

* * *

Keenyn

That nigga JJ didn't expect to see me at his door. As far as I knew he and Dame were still cool, but when he saw me his face fell. I was sure that was because he'd popped off on me the other night on the phone. He had no clue about me and Sen, or what I knew, so that wasn't it.

"What the fuck ya'll doin' here?" He asked holding the door open part way as he peered out at us standing on the porch.

Dame shook his head. "Let us in yo'. What the fuck? We yo' niggas."

JJ shook his head. "Nah, that mufucka ain't my nigga." He cut his eye at me.

"What nigga? 'Cause I ain't front you no weed? That's how the fuck you feel?"

Dame spoke up. "Don't be on that shit JJ. You know you and that nigga been boys since elementary school. It ain't like ya'll ain't never had no words before. Let that shit go. It's petty."

"Right," I agreed. "I'm over that shit man. I got a lot of shit goin' on and I said some shit I ain't mean."

JJ still seemed reluctant to let us in, but Dame pushed that nigga aside and I followed.

"Nigga, you trippin' yo!" JJ said trying to run in front of us. He closed an open door and led us down to the basement.

What the fuck was he trying to hide? The look that Dame gave me asked the same question.

"Sup wit' you nigga? Why you actin' all jumpy and shit?" My curiosity was peeked, so I had to ask.

"I know right. What nigga? You got a dead body in there or something?" Dame asked in a joking way, but damn he was really acting strange.

"Nah," JJ said quickly as we sat down. "It's just junky as fuck in there and shit. My son was here yesterday and I ain't cleaned up."

"Well damn nigga, since when you give a fuck if this mufucka's clean?" I had to laugh about that one.

"I know. Nasty ass nigga," Dame spat.

When I finally took a good look at JJ I noticed that he had on a pair of brand new red and black retro 13 Jordan's. Not only that, but his True Religion outfit looked fresh too. It wasn't even some shit that he'd borrowed from me. I wondered if he'd been in Dame's closet, but Dame shut that down.

"Damn man, you on yo' hustle ain't you?" Dame asked. "Nice kicks."

"Yeah man. You know. I got bills to pay and my bitch ain't fuckin' wit' no broke nigga." JJ chuckled and fidgeted in his seat like he was uncomfortable.

Something was up with that nigga.

"I hear that," Dame chuckled right along with him.

I wasn't laughing though.

"I gotta pee," I said and got up to head to the hallway bathroom.

The plan was for me to check to see what the hell was in that room. From what I remembered about that nigga's spot, that was a bedroom.

"Use the bathroom upstairs man. I'on know what that lil' nigga put in the toilet, but that shit won't flush." The look on JJ's face told me that he was really trying to hide something

"It ain't like I'm 'bout to take a shit nigga," I said jokingly.

"I'm just sayin' nigga. My girl's funny. She gon' flip if it smell like piss in there and shit," JJ sounded all nervous as he spoke.

"Whatever nigga." I walked out of the room and went upstairs like he'd advised me.

On the way down I tiptoed toward the door that he'd closed. At that moment that nigga JJ walked up the steps that led to the basement.

"You want a beer man?" He asked, which made me walk away from the door. I was pissed as hell.

"Yeah, I'll take a beer," I obliged before heading back down to the basement.

"You go in that room?" Dame asked.

"Nah, that nigga's actin' suspicious as fuck. I say we stop playin' nice and go ahead and get that nigga talkin'."

Dame nodded. "I was thinkin' the same thing. I just needed his guard down so he'd let us in."

JJ returned to the basement with three Coronas and a blunt that was already rolled. He lit it up and it smelled just like my shit.

"Damn man. Yo' smokin' ass still got some of that OZ left?" Dame asked with his hand lowering toward his waist.

JJ was so into his blunt that he didn't even notice as he placed the beers on the coffee table.

When he looked up Dame had his gun in his face. "What the fuck's goin' on wit' you nigga? Since when you and Trell been cool?"

"Nigga, it ain't even like that. Don't take that shit personal ya'll. I need a come up and Trell was willin' to help me. Unlike ya'll niggas. Ya'll s'posed to be my boys, but all ya'll do is down me and talk shit."

I couldn't help but laugh. "You think that fuck nigga wanted to help you? You one stupid ass nigga."

"How ya'll know anyway? I…know ya'll don't fuck wit' Trell." Sweat was starting to bead on JJ's forehead and nose.

"You scared nigga?" Dame taunted him. "Where's the video?"

"What video?" JJ's voice was trembling.

"You know exactly what video I'm talkin' 'bout. Where the fuck is it?" Dame used the butt of the gun to bust him in the forehead.

The blow opened his skin and blood started to pour down his face.

"Go see what was in that room while I find out what this fuck nigga knows."

I was thinking the same thing and as soon as he suggested it I was heading back up the steps. Although I wanted to know what JJ was saying, I really wanted to know what the fuck was in that damn room. When I swung the door open my mouth fell open and I made my way back down to the basement with my own gun drawn.

"Fuck that! I'm 'bout to kill this fuck nigga!" My gun was at his temple as Dame gave me a questioning look.

"Man wait. This nigga 'bout to tell me where the damn video is. Shit, calm the fuck down."

I was fuming as I breathed all hard. "Fuck that! I found at least ten bricks of Kush on the bed in that damn room. It's packaged exactly how I do my shit. That nigga took my shit! How the fuck you know where I keep my stash nigga?"

Tears were falling down JJ's cheeks. He was acting like a straight bitch, but having two guns in your face when you got caught up in your shit could do that to a nigga.

"Dame told me," he snitched.

Dame looked at me. "It wasn't like that man…I forgot that shit even slipped outta my mouth to that nigga."

"Was you in on that shit?" I had to know.

"Hell fuck no nigga. If I was in on it I wouldn't be here right now!"

I was ready to blow JJ's brains out, but we needed that damn video first.

"How many other mufuckas got that video nigga?" I asked JJ. For some reason I believed Dame.

"As far as I know I'm the only one. You pissed me off Keys. That's the only reason I took yo' shit. You can take it back. I'll give ya'll the video. Just don't kill me or tell Trell…I'll tell ya'll everything."

I laughed hard as fuck. That nigga must've been smoking something other than weed if he thought that shit was going to be that easy.

"I can take my shit back? Nigga, you funny as hell. Damn right I'm takin' my shit back. Not only are we takin' my shit back, but we takin' the video and we gon' take yo' life too!" I wasn't playing with his ass.

Because of him I was mad as hell at my pops. I was even plotting on that nigga and his girl. It crossed my mind that Kelly really wanted to fuck me and it had nothing to do with my weed getting stolen. Damn, that was fucked up. That hoe was really willing to fuck her own man's son. Trifling ass thot bitch.

"Please don't…please. We been boys since we were kids man." Dame begged.

"Let's just kill this cry bitch ass nigga," I said. "We'll ransack this mufucka 'till we find what we lookin' for."

"No, I'll tell you what you want to know. Just don't kill me," he pleaded, but his pleas fell on deaf ears.

Dame gave me a look that told me to go along with acting like we'd spare his life, so I backed down.

"A'ight. Where's the fuckin' video nigga?" Dame asked as I just looked on with venom in my eyes.

"It's in a shoebox in my closet in my bedroom."

I left the room and ran up to his bedroom. There were a lot of shoe boxes but only one of them had a DVD in it with no writing on it. There was no way for me to know if it was the right one by looking at it, so I looked around until I spotted a laptop on the bed. There was a password on that shit and that only added to my frustration.

"Damnit! Shit! Fuck!" I yelled before running back down to the basement.

When I spotted a desktop computer in the corner I made my way over to it and turned it on. Dame was still holding the gun on JJ who was still begging him not to kill him. I blocked all of that shit out as I waited for the computer to boot up. There was no password. Once it was on the home screen I found the CD Rom and opened it. I placed the DVD inside and pressed play after it closed.

Sure enough, it was what we were looking for. I removed the DVD and walked over to JJ. I pointed my gun at his head again.

"Are you the one that Trell got to watch Sen while he's gone?" I asked.

"Who is Sen and how ya'll niggas know so much?" I could tell that he didn't recognize that name.

"Jasenia, Mendosa's daughter."

"Oh, nah. He ain't tell me to watch her."

I nodded. "Okay. Did he tell you everything we need to know?" That question was for Dame.

Dame nodded. "Yeah, we done wit' him."

"Good." I turned my attention back to JJ. "I would've let you live, but you stole my shit nigga."

Pow! Pow!

I let two rounds off and turned to leave the room before his body could even fall. Shit, all I wanted was my ten bricks back. That snake ass nigga got exactly what he deserved. Before we left we packed my shit up in a bag that I'd found in the bedroom's closet. Then we made it look like a robbery by trashing the place. After that I made sure to put another DVD in the shoebox to throw Trell off just in case he came looking for it. Once he found out that JJ was dead, I was sure that he'd look to see if it was there. That would throw off any suspicion that Sen was in on the murder. I just hoped he didn't watch it before I killed him.

* * *

Jasenia

"I'm on my way over. I miss you." I told Keys over the phone.

It had been at least a week and a half since Trell had left for Savannah. I didn't know who he had watching me, but I was trying to be careful since we knew that it wasn't JJ.

I was aware of the fact that JJ was dead and was just grateful that at least we had one of the videos in our possession. Things had still been kind of different between me and Keys, but I was working on getting us back to where we were.

It was my idea to go back to my condo. I needed things to seem normal just in case someone was really watching me for Trell. Knowing that Keys was never too far away was comforting. He was scared that somebody would be coming after me although Trell was gone, so he kept a close eye on me too. So far nothing out of the ordinary had happened. The only places I went were to my father's house and back home. I hadn't seen Keys since the day I left, although we talked on the phone constantly.

"Okay, but be careful," he simply said before hanging up.

I grabbed my purse, walked out of the side door and down the street. I'd already accessed my Uber app and gave the address of a nearby Burger King. Anybody that Trell had watching me wouldn't have ever thought I'd be walking, let alone waiting at a Burger King for Uber.

In less than an hour I was where I wanted to be. I knocked on the door and waited to see his handsome face. When he opened the door his reaction surprised me.

"Hey," he said and stepped aside without hugging me or giving me a kiss.

After he closed the door I had to ask, "What the hell Keys? You've been actin' funny for a minute. What's the problem?"

"I don't wanna come across as wantin' too much too soon," he threw my words back in my face.

"Oh, so that's what this is all about? I didn't mean it the way you took it."

I followed him and sat down on the sofa. He didn't say anything, so I did. "I only meant that you want me to reveal everything about me in such a short amount of time. Just like you said before, we don't know each other as adults. I love you Keys and I don't want to push you away by letting you know about every little fucked up fragment of me."

"You gave me your heart and your body though Sen." He shook his head. "See, that's yo' problem yo'. Instead of being real and keepin' shit one hundred yo' ass is so worried about losin' somebody. I ain't gon' leave you and yo' pops ain't either. You gotta stop worryin' about what we think. When a person loves you none of that bullshit matters. You see how I'm willin' to murk a nigga for you. C'mon, why the fuck you doubtin' me? I'm here. I ain't goin' nowhere...no matter what. Kill that shit ma."

I shivered with desire at how he took control. He wasn't controlling like Trell though. Instead of being violent and disrespectful with it, Keys was more thoughtful. He was only demanding because he really gave a fuck about me.

Without saying anything to spoil the moment, I simply undressed and stood in front of him with my heels still on.

"Didn't I say I missed you baby?"

He shook his head and closed the distance between us.

"See, here you go wit' that sexy ass shit."

I gave him a sly, but lustful look. "Shut up and kiss me."

He did, but when he pulled away his facial expression matched mine. My man was turned on.

"I got other plans for you," he said as he scooped me up in his arms and carried me to the bed.

Of course he had to partake in his favorite pastime and eat me all good first. When he entered me I came instantly.

"Damn," I breathed as I held on to him.

I was on top, but he was obviously in control.

"Tell me you love me," he demanded.

"I love you Keys..."

* * *

The sound of shouting woke me up from the most peaceful sleep I'd had in a while. At first I thought Keys was in the living room watching television, but the voice that was yelling sounded familiar. I jumped out of the bed butt naked and realized that I had to throw on some clothes. I found my shorts and a t-shirt that I normally slept in and tiptoed out into the hallway. When I peeked around the corner what I saw shocked the hell out of me.

"What the fuck?" I reacted.

They both looked at me with guns pointed at each other's heads.

"I knew she was here!" My father growled in anger. "Are you fuckin' my daughter nigga! I ain't gon' ask you again." He cocked the gun and I rushed over to stop him before he killed the man I loved.

I grabbed his arm. "Daddy, please, just calm down. It's not what you think!"

"That's the same shit that nigga said."

Keys just glowered at him proving that he wasn't afraid. If he killed my father, I didn't know how I'd be able to forgive him. Then again, if my father killed him, I wouldn't be able to forgive him either.

"Because it's true. Please, put the gun down…" I looked at Keys. "Both of you."

They were both being hard asses because neither of them seemed to be listening to me.

"I said put the fuckin' guns down!" I screamed at the top of my lungs. "If you two give a fuck about me you'll think about me and how I feel about this shit! Not just how you feel!"

They both slowly lowered their guns, but the hostility was still thick in the room.

"What the hell's going on Sen?" My father's voice was finally a little bit calmer, but fury was clear in his dark eyes.

"How'd you know I was here?" I asked.

"I didn't really know that shit for sure. It was just...a feelin' I had. Call it father's intuition. The way you were lookin' at each and shit. It was naggin' me. Then that nigga was actin' all strange when he copped the other day. Like he was hidin' some shit. I stopped by your condo first, because I been worried about you for some reason. Something told me you was fuckin' wit' this nigga. Keys man, how you gon' fuck my daughter nigga? You know how I feel about my only daughter." His teeth were clenched as he talked.

Keys paced the floor and then rubbed his free hand across his head over and over. "I ain't plan this Mendosa. I ain't just...fuckin' yo' daughter yo'. I love her."

"Oh my God, so ya'll *are* fuckin'," Mendosa groaned miserably. "Shit!" He pointed the gun at Keys. "I should kill you right now!"

"Daddy no! Please! I love him..." I couldn't hold the tears back. "Because of him I'm alive. Please, just...just listen to me."

He lowered the gun again and turned to look at me. "Yeah, he mentioned protectin' you. Is somebody tryna kill you? Why didn't you just come to me? You know I'll protect you from anything. You fuckin' know that Sen."

I shook my head. "No daddy. This is different. I knew you'd be mad at me. You're the only person who loves me…well other than Keys… and I didn't want you to stop loving me."

"Just talk to me baby girl." His eyes were suddenly softer, but that gun was still in his hand. "I'll never stop lovin' you."

"Uh, can you put that away?" I asked nervously.

"If that nigga put his away," he said cutting his eye at Keys.

Keys tucked the gun in his waistband and finally sat down on the sofa. I guess he was just glad I was going to tell my father the truth finally. My father put his gun away too and I went ahead and confessed.

"I've been seein' Trell. Uh, he was my boyfriend. Well, technically he still is…"

"Oh hell nah!" My father really went off then. "Please tell me you didn't. You didn't fuck him too did you? I'm confused right now Sen. You wit' Keys, but you wit' Trell too? What happened to my little angel? Shit! Didn't I tell you to stay away from Trell! Huh! I told you that shit for a reason Sen! Fuck!" He acted like he wanted to fuck some shit up, but he kept his self-control the best he could.

"I was pissed because you were with Sybil. I wanted to get back at you somehow. I'm so sorry daddy." I explained what Trell had planned and the video that he had of him killing his father. "Why'd you kill him?"

Suddenly my father's whole demeanor changed. He let out a sigh as he took a seat on the love seat across from where Keys was sitting. He ran his hand over his face as he seemed to contemplate what to say next. I figured that the news about Keys and Trell was enough for now. I'd eventually let him in on what I'd done to lead to Will's murder.

"Boss was my nigga," he started. I was aware that Boss was Trell's father. "We took over the game together, but over the years we seemed to drift apart. He called me out of the blue one night and told me he needed to talk. I got in my car and went straight to his crib. Shit, I wasn't thinkin' 'bout no damn surveillance camera. I knew that he had them all over the property, but when I get mad 'bout some shit I don't give a fuck 'bout no consequences. When I got there that nigga confronted me time I got out of the car 'bout fuckin' his wife. He told me that he knew everything and he was gon' tell Melissa to keep you away from me. Then he said he had fucked Melissa too. That shit made me snap. I had my gun on me, but I wanted to kill him wit' my bare hands. As I'm chokin' him out he tells me that he knows that Trell is mine 'cause he was locked up when Angela got pregnant. I couldn't chance him tellin' your mother anything…"

"Is it true…were you fuckin' his mother? Could he be your…son?" My voice was faint and I felt sick to my stomach. Was it possible that Trell could be my brother? Could that shit really be true?

He looked up at me and I saw the truth in his eyes before he even confirmed it. The bile rose up to my throat and I jumped up to make it to the bathroom. Oh my God, I'd fucked my brother. I couldn't believe that shit. That was why my father was so adamant about hating Trell and keeping me away from him. Suddenly everything made sense. As I retched I cried my eyes out. I was really going to hell. Fuck! As if shit could get any worse.

* * *

Keenyn

The shock of what Mendosa had revealed had got to me too, but I got up to check on Sen. I held her hair back as she threw up in the toilet. She was on her knees and she was also crying as she vomited.

"Baby, you gotta calm down before you choke yourself."

Her voice was weak. "I fucked my brother Keys."

"You didn't know."

I heard Mendosa walk up behind us. "I'm sorry Sen. I never wanted the truth to come out."

"Does he know that he's my brother?" She asked.

"No," Mendosa answered.

"He doesn't look like you," Sen whined.

"He looks like his mother."

"You know that he's your son one hundred percent?" Sen asked still not wanting to believe it. "I mean, if she fucked you who knows who else she fucked."

"I'm at least ninety percent sure," Mendosa confirmed.

"So Angela went crazy after Boss was killed right?" I asked.

"Nah, she didn't love Boss. She was glad he was dead. She went crazy because I didn't want to be with her. After I killed him, I got rid of his body by feedin' it to some hogs. My nigga got a hog farm in Macon. Hogs will eat anything. Even bones and hair. My ass never thought to go back and get the video. That was messy, but after so many years had went by, I thought that shit would never come back up."

Once Sen was done and she was only dry heaving, I managed to help her up. She brushed her teeth and I just stood there and watched her. I felt so helpless. I couldn't protect her from herself.

"You gon' be okay? I'm gon' talk to yo' pops."

She nodded, but her sad eyes told it all.

Me and Mendosa walked off to the living room.

"I need you to help me get rid of that nigga." I filled him in on the plan, the bug and Trell's visit to see his mom in Savannah.

Mendosa nodded. "I'm gon' help you 'cause she's my daughter and it's my fault she's goin' through this. Just know that I still wanna kill you Keys. The only reason yo' ass is still alive is 'cuz she claims she loves you, but any wrong move nigga and yo' life and yo' father's life is over. Got it."

Because of my love for her, I had to respect what her pops had said, although it would never be that easy to kill me. Not even for Mendosa.

"Yeah man, but what's really important right now is makin' sure we kill yo' son." There was an evil smirk on my face and it was clear that he felt my wrath.

"Yeah nigga, just don't hurt my fuckin' daughter. You hurt her, you get hurt...permanently."

The threats were enough, but I was already prepared for Mendosa. I wasn't going nowhere, because Sen was mine. He'd get over it in time, but for now, what was most important was keeping the woman that we both loved alive.

The End...for now...
Part two is coming soon and it will be the finale.

The Plug's Daughter   Nika Michelle

91753304R00126

Made in the USA
Middletown, DE
02 October 2018